MISS BILLY

ELEANOR H. PORTER

Miss Billy

Eleanor H. Porter

© 1st World Library, 2009
PO Box 2211
Fairfield, IA 52556
www.1stworldlibrary.com
First Edition

LCCN: 2009923377

Softcover ISBN: 978-1-4218-8827-9
Hardcover ISBN: 978-1-4218-8926-9
eBook ISBN: 978-1-4218-8728-9

Purchase *"Miss Billy"*
as a traditional bound book at:
www.1stWorldLibrary.com/purchase.asp?ISBN=978-1-4218-8827-9

1st World Library is a literary, educational organization
dedicated to:

- Creating a free internet library of downloadable ebooks

- Hosting writing competitions and offering book publishing
  scholarships.

Interested in more 1st World Library books? contact:
literacy@1stworldlibrary.com
Check us out at: www.1stworldlibrary.com

1ˢᵗ World Library Literary Society

Giving Back to the World

"If you want to work on the core problem, it's early school literacy."

- James Barksdale, former CEO of Netscape

"No skill is more crucial to the future of a child, or to a democratic and prosperous society, than literacy."

- Los Angeles Times

"Literacy... means far more than learning how to read and write... The aim is to transmit... knowledge and promote social participation."

- UNESCO

"Literacy is not a luxury, it is a right and a responsibility. If our world is to meet the challenges of the twenty-first century we must harness the energy and creativity of all our citizens."

- President Bill Clinton

"Parents should be encouraged to read to their children, and teachers should be equipped with all available techniques for teaching literacy, so the varying needs and capacities of individual kids can be taken into account."

- Hugh Mackay

CONTENTS

CHAPTER I

BILLY WRITES A LETTER

Billy Neilson was eighteen years old when the aunt, who had brought her up from babyhood, died. Miss Benton's death left Billy quite alone in the world—alone, and peculiarly forlorn. To Mr. James Harding, of Harding & Harding, who had charge of Billy's not inconsiderable property, the girl poured out her heart in all its loneliness two days after the funeral.

"You see, Mr. Harding, there isn't any one—not any one who —cares," she choked.

"Tut, tut, my child, it's not so bad as that, surely," remonstrated the old man, gently. "Why, I—I care."

Billy smiled through tear-wet eyes.

"But I can't LIVE with you," she said.

"I'm not so sure of that, either," retorted the man. "I'm thinking that Letty and Ann would LIKE to have you with us."

The girl laughed now outright. She was thinking of Miss Letty, who had "nerves," and of Miss Ann, who had a "heart"; and she pictured her own young, breezy, healthy self attempting to conform to the hushed and shaded thing that life was, within Lawyer Harding's home.

"Thank you, but I'm sure they wouldn't," she objected. "You don't know how noisy I am."

The lawyer stirred restlessly and pondered.

"But, surely, my dear, isn't there some relative, somewhere?" he demanded. "How about your mother's people?"

Billy shook her head. Her eyes filled again with tears.

"There was only Aunt Ella, ever, that I knew anything about. She and mother were the only children there were, and mother died when I was a year old, you know."

"But your father's people?"

"It's even worse there. He was an only child and an orphan when mother married him. He died when I was but six months old. After that there was only mother and Aunt Ella, then Aunt Ella alone; and now—no one."

"And you know nothing of your father's people?"

"Nothing; that is—almost nothing."

"Then there is some one?"

Billy smiled. A deeper pink showed in her cheeks.

"Why, there's one—a man but he isn't really father's people, anyway. But I—I have been tempted to write to him."

Eleanor H. Porter

"Who is he?"

"The one I'm named for. He was father's boyhood chum. You see that's why I'm 'Billy' instead of being a proper 'Susie,' or 'Bessie,' or 'Sally Jane.' Father had made up his mind to name his baby 'William' after his chum, and when I came, Aunt Ella said, he was quite broken-hearted until somebody hit upon the idea of naming me Billy.' Then he was content, for it seems that he always called his chum 'Billy' anyhow. And so—'Billy' I am to-day."

"Do you know this man?"

"No. You see father died, and mother and Aunt Ella knew him only very slightly. Mother knew his wife, though, Aunt Ella said, and SHE was lovely."

"Hm—; well, we might look them up, perhaps. You know his address?"

"Oh, yes unless he's moved. We've always kept that. Aunt Ella used to say sometimes that she was going to write to him some day about me, you know."

"What's his name?"

"William Henshaw. He lives in Boston."

Lawyer Harding snatched off his glasses, and leaned forward in his chair.

"William Henshaw! Not the Beacon Street Henshaws!" he cried.

It was Billy's turn to be excited. She, too, leaned forward eagerly.

"Oh, do you know him? That's lovely! And his address IS Beacon Street! I know because I saw it only to-day. You see, I HAVE been tempted to write him."

"Write him? Of course you'll write him," cried the lawyer. "And we don't need to do much 'looking up' there, child. I've known the family for years, and this William was a college mate of my boy's. Nice fellow, too. I've heard Ned speak of him. There were three sons, William, and two others much younger than he. I've forgotten their names."

"Then you do know him! I'm so glad," exclaimed Billy. "You see, he never seemed to me quite real."

"I know about him," corrected the lawyer, smilingly, "though I'll confess I've rather lost track of him lately. Ned will know. I'll ask Ned. Now go home, my dear, and dry those pretty eyes of yours. Or, better still, come home with me to tea. I—I'll telephone up to the house." And he rose stiffly and went into the inner office.

Some minutes passed before he came back, red of face, and plainly distressed.

"My dear child, I—I'm sorry, but—but I'll have to take back that invitation," he blurted out miserably. "My sisters are— are not well this afternoon. Ann has been having a turn with her heart—you know Ann's heart is—is bad; and Letty— Letty is always nervous at such times—very nervous. Er— I'm so sorry! But you'll—excuse it?"

"Indeed I will," smiled Billy, "and thank you just the same; only"—her eyes twinkled mischievously—"you don't mind if I do say that it IS lucky that we hadn't gone on planning to have me live with them, Mr. Harding!"

Eleanor H. Porter

"Eh? Well—er, I think your plan about the Henshaws is very good," he interposed hurriedly. "I'll speak to Ned—I'll speak to Ned," he finished, as he ceremoniously bowed the girl from the office.

James Harding kept his word, and spoke to his son that night; but there was little, after all, that Ned could tell him. Yes, he remembered Billy Henshaw well, but he had not heard of him for years, since Henshaw's marriage, in fact. He must be forty years old, Ned said; but he was a fine fellow, an exceptionally fine fellow, and would be sure to deal kindly and wisely by his little orphan namesake; of that Ned was very sure.

"That's good. I'll write him," declared Mr. James Harding. "I'll write him tomorrow."

He did write—but not so soon as Billy wrote; for even as he spoke, Billy, in her lonely little room at the other end of the town, was laying bare all her homesickness in four long pages to "Dear Uncle William."

CHAPTER II

"THE STRATA"

Bertram Henshaw called the Beacon Street home "The Strata." This annoyed Cyril, and even William, not a little; though they reflected that, after all, it was "only Bertram." For the whole of Bertram's twenty-four years of life it had been like this—"It's only Bertram," had been at once the curse and the salvation of his existence.

In this particular case, however, Bertram's vagary of fancy had some excuse. The Beacon Street house, the home of the three brothers, was a "Strata."

"You see, it's like this," Bertram would explain airily to some new acquaintance who expressed surprise at the name; "if I could slice off the front of the house like a loaf of cake, you'd understand it better. But just suppose that old Bunker Hill should suddenly spout fire and brimstone and bury us under tons of ashes—only fancy the condition of mind of those future archaeologists when they struck our house after their months of digging!

"What would they find? Listen. First: stratum number one, the top floor; that's Cyril's, you know. They'd note the bare floors, the sparse but heavy furniture, the piano, the violin,

Eleanor H. Porter

the flute, the book-lined walls, and the absence of every sort of curtain, cushion, or knickknack. 'Here lived a plain man,' they'd say; 'a scholar, a musician, stern, unloved and unloving; a monk.'

"And what next? They'd strike William's stratum next, the third floor. Imagine it! You know William as a State Street broker, well-off, a widower, tall, angular, slow of speech, a little bald, very much nearsighted, and the owner of the kindest heart in the world. But really to know William, you must know his rooms. William collects things. He has always collected things—and he's saved every one of them. There's a tradition that at the age of one year he crept into the house with four small round white stones. Anyhow, if he did, he's got them now. Rest assured of that—and he's forty this year. Miniatures, carved ivories, bugs, moths, porcelains, jades, stamps, postcards, spoons, baggage tags, theatre programs, playing-cards—there isn't anything that he doesn't collect. He's on teapots, now. Imagine it—William and teapots! And they're all there in his rooms—one glorious mass of confusion. Just fancy those archaeologists trying to make their 'monk' live there!

"But when they reach me, my stratum, they'll have a worse time yet. You see, *I* like cushions and comfort, and I have them everywhere. And I like—well, I like lots of things. My rooms don't belong to that monk, not a little bit. And so you see," Bertram would finish merrily, "that's why I call it all 'The Strata.'"

And "The Strata" it was to all the Henshaws' friends, and even to William and Cyril themselves, in spite of their objection to the term.

From babyhood the Henshaw boys had lived in the handsome, roomy house, facing the Public Garden. It had been their father's boyhood home, as well, and he and his wife had died there, soon after Kate, the only daughter, had married. At the age of twenty-two, William Henshaw, the eldest son, had brought his bride to the house, and together they had striven to make a home for the two younger orphan boys, Cyril, twelve, and Bertram, six. But Mrs. William, after a short five years of married life, had died; and since then, the house had known almost nothing of a woman's touch or care.

Little by little as the years passed, the house and its inmates had fallen into what had given Bertram his excuse for the name. Cyril, thirty years old now, dignified, reserved, averse to cats, dogs, women, and confusion, had early taken himself and his music to the peace and exclusiveness of the fourth floor. Below him, William had long discouraged any meddling with his precious chaos of possessions, and had finally come to spend nearly all his spare time among them. This left Bertram to undisputed ownership of the second floor, and right royally did he hold sway there with his paints and brushes and easels, his old armor, rich hangings, rugs, and cushions, and everywhere his specialty—his "Face of a Girl." From canvas, plaque, and panel they looked out— those girlish faces: winsome, wilful, pert, demure, merry, sad, beautiful, even almost ugly—they were all there; and they were growing famous, too. The world of art was beginning to take notice, and to adjust its spectacles for a more critical glance. This "Face of a Girl" by Henshaw bade fair to be worth while.

Below Bertram's cheery second floor were the dim old library and drawing-rooms, silent, stately, and almost never used; and below them were the dining-room and the kitchen. Here ruled Dong Ling, the Chinese cook, and Pete.

Pete was—indeed, it is hard telling what Pete was. He said

he was the butler; and he looked the part when he answered the bell at the great front door. But at other times, when he swept a room, or dusted Master William's curios, he looked—like nothing so much as what he was: a fussy, faithful old man, who expected to die in the service he had entered fifty years before as a lad.

Thus in all the Beacon Street house, there had not for years been the touch of a woman's hand. Even Kate, the married sister, had long since given up trying to instruct Dong Ling or to chide Pete, though she still walked across the Garden from her Commonwealth Avenue home and tripped up the stairs to call in turn upon her brothers, Bertram, William, and Cyril.

CHAPTER III

THE STRATA—WHEN THE LETTER COMES

It was on the six o'clock delivery that William Henshaw received the letter from his namesake, Billy. To say the least, the letter was a great shock to him. He had not quite forgotten Billy's father, who had died so long ago, it is true, but he had forgotten Billy, entirely. Even as he looked at the disconcerting epistle with its round, neatly formed letters, he had great difficulty in ferreting out the particular niche in his memory which contained the fact that Walter Neilson had had a child, and had named it for him.

And this child, this "Billy," this unknown progeny of an all but forgotten boyhood friend, was asking a home, and with him! Impossible! And William Henshaw peered at the letter as if, at this second reading, its message could not be so monstrous.

"Well, old man, what's up?" It was Bertram's amazed voice from the hall doorway; and indeed, William Henshaw, red-faced and plainly trembling, seated on the lowest step of the stairway, and gazing, wild-eyed, at the letter in his hand, was somewhat of an amazing sight. "What IS up?"

"What's up!" groaned William, starting to his feet, and

waving the letter frantically in the air. "What's up! Young man, do you want us to take in a child to board?—a CHILD?" he repeated in slow horror.

"Well, hardly," laughed the other. "Er, perhaps Cyril might like it, though; eh?"

"Come, come, Bertram, be sensible for once," pleaded his brother, nervously. "This is serious, really serious, I tell you!"

"What is serious?" demanded Cyril, coming down the stairway. "Can't it wait? Pete has already sounded the gong twice for dinner."

William made a despairing gesture.

"Well, come," he groaned. "I'll tell you at the table.... It seems I've got a namesake," he resumed in a shaking voice, a few moments later; "Walter Neilson's child."

"And who's Walter Neilson?" asked Bertram.

"A boyhood friend. You wouldn't remember him. This letter is from his child."

"Well, let's hear it. Go ahead. I fancy we can stand the— LETTER; eh, Cyril?"

Cyril frowned. Cyril did not know, perhaps, how often he frowned at Bertram.

The eldest brother wet his lips. His hand shook as he picked up the letter.

"It—it's so absurd," he muttered. Then he cleared his throat and read the letter aloud.

"DEAR UNCLE WILLIAM: Do you mind my calling you that? You see I want SOME one, and there isn't any one now. You are the nearest I've got. Maybe you've forgotten, but I'm named for you. Walter Neilson was my father, you know. My Aunt Ella has just died.

"Would you mind very much if I came to live with you? That is, between times—I'm going to college, of course, and after that I'm going to be—well, I haven't decided that part yet. I think I'll consult you. You may have some preference, you know. You can be thinking it up until I come.

"There! Maybe I ought not to have said that, for perhaps you won't want me to come. I AM noisy, I'll own, but not so I think you'll mind it much unless some of you have 'nerves' or a 'heart.' You see, Miss Letty and Miss Ann—they're Mr. Harding's sisters, and Mr. Harding is our lawyer, and he will write to you. Well, where was I? Oh, I know—on Miss Letty's nerves. And, say, do you know, that is where I do get—on Miss Letty's nerves. I do, truly. You see, Mr. Harding very kindly suggested that I live with them, but, mercy! Miss Letty's nerves won't let you walk except on tiptoe, and Miss Ann's heart won't let you speak except in whispers. All the chairs and tables have worn little sockets in the carpets, and it's a crime to move them. There isn't a window-shade in the house that isn't pulled down EXACTLY to the middle sash, except where the sun shines, and those are pulled way down. Imagine me and Spunk living there! Oh, by the way, you don't mind my bringing Spunk, do you? I hope you don't, for I couldn't live without Spunk, and he couldn't live with out me.

Eleanor H. Porter

"Please let me hear from you very soon. I don't mind if you telegraph; and just 'come' would be all you'd have to say. Then I'd get ready right away and let you know what train to meet me on. And, oh, say—if you'll wear a pink in your buttonhole I will, too. Then we'll know each other. My address is just 'Hampden Falls.'

"Your awfully homesick namesake,

"BILLY HENSHAW NEILSON"

For one long minute there was a blank silence about the Henshaw dinner-table; then the eldest brother, looking anxiously from one man to the other, stammered:

"W-well?"

"Great Scott!" breathed Bertram.

Cyril said nothing, but his lips were white with their tense pressure against each other.

There was another pause, and again William broke it anxiously.

"Boys, this isn't helping me out any! What's to be done?"

"'Done'!" flamed Cyril. "Surely, you aren't thinking for a moment of LETTING that child come here, William!"

Bertram chuckled.

"He WOULD liven things up, Cyril; wouldn't he? Such nice smooth floors you've got up-stairs to trundle little tin carts across!"

"Tin nonsense!" retorted Cyril. "Don't be silly, Bertram. That letter wasn't written by a baby. He'd be much more likely to make himself at home with your paint box, or with some of William's junk."

"Oh, I say," expostulated William, "we'll HAVE to keep him out of those things, you know."

Cyril pushed back his chair from the table.

"'We'll have to keep him out'! William, you can't be in earnest! You aren't going to let that boy come here," he cried.

"But what can I do?" faltered the man.

"Do? Say 'no,' of course. As if we wanted a boy to bring up!"

"But I must do something. I—I'm all he's got. He says so."

"Good heavens! Well, send him to boarding-school, then, or to the penitentiary; anywhere but here!"

"Shucks! Let the kid come," laughed Bertram. "Poor little homesick devil! What's the use? I'll take him in. How old is he, anyhow?"

William frowned, and mused aloud slowly.

"Why, I don't know. He must be—er—why, boys, he's no child," broke off the man suddenly. "Walter himself died seventeen or eighteen years ago, not more than a year or two after he was married. That child must be somewhere around eighteen years old!"

"And only think how Cyril WAS worrying about those tin

carts," laughed Bertram. "Never mind—eight or eighteen— let him come. If he's that age, he won't bother much."

"And this—er—'Spunk'; do you take him, too? But probably he doesn't bother, either," murmured Cyril, with smooth sarcasm.

"Gorry! I forgot Spunk," acknowledged Bertram. "Say, what in time is Spunk, do you suppose?"

"Dog, maybe," suggested William.

"Well, whatever he is, you will kindly keep Spunk down-stairs," said Cyril with decision. "The boy, I suppose I shall have to endure; but the dog—!"

"Hm-m; well, judging by his name," murmured Bertram, apologetically, "it may be just possible that Spunk won't be easily controlled. But maybe he isn't a dog, anyhow. He— er—sounds something like a parrot to me."

Cyril rose to his feet abruptly. He had eaten almost no dinner.

"Very well," he said coldly. "But please remember that I hold you responsible, Bertram. Whether it's a dog, or a parrot, or—or a monkey, I shall expect you to keep Spunk down-stairs. This adopting into the family an unknown boy seems to me very absurd from beginning to end. But if you and William will have it so, of course I've nothing to say. Fortunately my rooms are at the TOP of the house," he finished, as he turned and left the dining-room.

For a moment there was silence. The brows of the younger man were uplifted quizzically.

"I'm afraid Cyril is bothered," murmured William then, in a troubled voice.

Bertram's face changed. Stern lines came to his boyish mouth.

"He is always bothered—with anything, lately."

The elder man sighed.

"I know, but with his talent—"

"'Talent'! Great Scott!" cut in Bertram. "Half the world has talent of one sort or another; but that doesn't necessarily make them unable to live with any one else! Really, Will, it's becoming serious—about Cyril. He's getting to be, for all the world, like those finicky old maids that that young namesake of yours wrote about. He'll make us whisper and walk on tiptoe yet!"

The other smiled.

"Don't you worry. You aren't in any danger of being kept too quiet, young man."

"No thanks to Cyril, then," retorted Bertram. "Anyhow, that's one reason why I was for taking the kid—to mellow up Cyril. He needs it all right."

"But I had to take him, Bert," argued the elder brother, his face growing anxious again. "But Heaven only knows what I'm going to do with him when I get him. What shall I say to him, anyway? How shall I write? I don't know how to get up a letter of that sort!"

"Why not take him at his word and telegraph? I fancy you

Eleanor H. Porter

won't have to say 'come' but once before you see him. He doesn't seem to be a bashful youth."

"Hm-m; I might do that," acquiesced William, slowly. "But wasn't there somebody—a lawyer—going to write to me?" he finished, consulting the letter by his plate. "Yes," he added, after a moment, "a Mr. Harding. Wonder if he's any relation to Ned Harding. I used to know Ned at Harvard, and seems as if he came from Hampden Falls. We'll soon see, at all events. Maybe I'll hear to-morrow."

"I shouldn't wonder," nodded Bertram, as he rose from the table. "Anyhow, I wouldn't do anything till I did hear."

CHAPTER IV

BILLY SENDS A TELEGRAM

James Harding's letter very promptly followed Billy's, though it was not like Billy's at all. It told something of Billy's property, and mentioned that, according to Mrs. Neilson's will, Billy would not come into control of her fortune until the age of twenty-one years was reached. It dwelt at some length upon the fact of Billy's loneliness in the world, and expressed the hope that her father's friend could find it in his heart to welcome the orphan into his home. It mentioned Ned, and the old college friendship, and it closed by saying that the writer, James Harding, was glad to renew his acquaintance with the good old Henshaw family that he had known long years ago; and that he hoped soon to hear from William Henshaw himself.

It was a good letter—but it was not well written. James Harding's handwriting was not distinguished for its legibility, and his correspondents rejoiced that the most of his letters were dictated to his stenographer. In this case, however, he had elected to use the more personal pen; and it was because of this that William Henshaw, even after reading the letter, was still unaware of his mistake in supposing his namesake, Billy, to be a boy.

In the main the lawyer had referred to Billy by name, or as "the orphan," or as that "poor, lonely child." And whenever the more distinctive feminine "her" or "herself" had occurred, the carelessly formed letters had made them so much like "his" and "himself" that they carried no hint of the truth to a man who had not the slightest reason for thinking himself in the wrong. It was therefore still for the "boy," Billy, that William Henshaw at once set about making a place in the home.

First he telegraphed the single word "Come" to Billy.

"I'll set the poor lad's heart at rest," he said to Bertram. "I shall answer Harding's letter more at length, of course. Naturally he wants to know something about me now before he sends Billy along; but there is no need for the boy to wait before he knows that I'll take him. Of course he won't come yet, till Harding hears from me."

It was just here, however, that William Henshaw met with a surprise, for within twenty-four hours came Billy's answer, and by telegraph.

"I'm coming to-morrow. Train due at five P. M.

"BILLY."

William Henshaw did not know that in Hampden Falls Billy's trunk had been packed for days. Billy was desperate. The house, even with the maid, and with the obliging neighbor and his wife who stayed there nights, was to Billy nothing but a dismal tomb. Lawyer Harding had fallen suddenly ill; she could not even tell him that the blessed telegram "Come" had arrived. Hence Billy, lonely, impulsive, and always used to pleasing herself, had taken matters in hand with a confident grasp, and had determined to wait no longer.

That it was a fearsomely unknown future to which she was so jauntily pledging herself did not trouble the girl in the least. Billy was romantic. To sally gaily forth with a pink in the buttonhole of her coat to find her father's friend who was a "Billy" too, seemed to Billy Neilson not only delightful, but eminently sensible, and an excellent way out of her present homesick loneliness. So she bought the pink and her ticket, and impatiently awaited the time to start.

To the Beacon Street house, Billy's cheerful telegram brought the direst consternation. Even Kate was hastily summoned to the family conclave that immediately resulted.

"There's nothing—simply nothing that I can do," she declared irritably, when she had heard the story. "Surely, you don't expect ME to take the boy!"

"No, no, of course not," sighed William. "But you see, I supposed I'd have time to—to get used to things, and to make arrangements; and this is so—so sudden! I hadn't even answered Harding's letter until to-day; and he hasn't got that—much less replied to it."

"But what could you expect after sending that idiotic telegram?" demanded the lady. "'Come,' indeed!"

"But that's what Billy told me to do."

"What if it was? Just because a foolish eighteen-year-old boy tells you to do something, must you, a supposedly sensible forty-year-old man obey?"

"I think it tickled Will's romantic streak," laughed Bertram. "It seemed so sort of alluring to send that one word 'Come' out into space, and watch what happened."

"Well, he's found out, certainly," observed Cyril, with grim satisfaction.

"Oh, no; it hasn't happened yet," corrected Bertram, cheerfully. "It's just going to happen. William's got to put on the pink first, you know. That's the talisman."

William reddened.

"Bertram, don't be foolish. I sha'n't wear any pink. You must know that."

"How'll you find him, then?"

"Why, he'll have one on; that's enough," settled William.

"Hm-m; maybe. Then he'll have Spunk, too," murmured Bertram, mischievously.

"Spunk!" cried Kate.

"Yes. He wrote that he hoped we wouldn't mind his bringing Spunk with him."

"Who's Spunk?

"We don't know." Bertram's lips twitched.

"You don't know! What do you mean?"

"Well, Will thinks it's a dog, and I believe Cyril is anticipating a monkey. I myself am backing it for a parrot."

"Boys, what have you done!" groaned Kate, falling back in

her chair. "What have you done!"

To William her words were like an electric shock stirring him to instant action. He sprang abruptly to his feet.

"Well, whatever we've done, we've done it," he declared sternly; "and now we must do the rest—and do it well, too. He's the son of my boyhood's dearest friend, and he shall be made welcome. Now to business! Bertram, you said you'd take him in. Did you mean it?"

Bertram sobered instantly, and came erect in his chair. William did not often speak like this; but when he did—

"Yes, Will. He shall have the little bedroom at the end of the hall. I never used the room much, anyhow, and what few duds I have there shall be cleared out to-morrow."

"Good! Now there are some other little details to arrange, then I'll go down-stairs and tell Pete and Dong Ling. And, please to understand, we're going to make this lad welcome—welcome, I say!"

"Yes, sir," said Bertram. Neither Kate nor Cyril spoke.

Eleanor H. Porter

CHAPTER V

GETTING READY FOR BILLY

The Henshaw household was early astir on the day of Billy's expected arrival, and preparations for the guest's comfort were well under way before breakfast. The center of activity was in the little room at the end of the hall on the second floor; though, as Bertram said, the whole Strata felt the "upheaval."

By breakfast time Bertram with the avowed intention of giving "the little chap half a show," had the room cleared for action; and after that the whole house was called upon for contributions toward the room's adornment. And most generously did most of the house respond. Even Dong Ling slippered up-stairs and presented a weird Chinese banner which he said he was "velly much glad" to give. As to Pete—Pete was in his element. Pete loved boys. Had he not served them nearly all his life? Incidentally it may be mentioned that he did not care for girls.

Only Cyril held himself aloof. But that he was not oblivious of the proceedings below him was evidenced by the somber bass that floated down from his piano strings. Cyril always played according to the mood that was on him; and when Bertram heard this morning the rhythmic beats of mournfulness, he chuckled and said to William:

"That's Chopin's Funeral March. Evidently Cy thinks this is the death knell to all his hopes of future peace and happiness."

"Dear me! I wish Cyril would take some interest," grieved William.

"Oh, he takes interest all right," laughed Bertram, meaningly. "He takes INTEREST!"

"I know, but—Bertram," broke off the elder man, anxiously, from his perch on the stepladder, "would you put the rifle over this window, or the fishing-rod?"

"Why, I don't think it makes much difference, so long as they're somewhere," answered Bertram. "And there are these Indian clubs and the swords to be disposed of, you know."

"Yes; and it's going to look fine; don't you think?" exulted William. "And you know for the wall-space between the windows I'm going to bring down that case of mine, of spiders."

Bertram raised his hands in mock surprise.

"Here—down here! You're going to trust any of those precious treasures of yours down here!"

William frowned.

"Nonsense, Bertram, don't be silly! They'll be safe enough. Besides, they're old, anyhow. I was on spiders years ago—when I was Billy's age, in fact. I thought he'd like them here. You know boys always like such things."

Eleanor H. Porter

"Oh, 'twasn't Billy I was worrying about," retorted Bertram. "It was you—and the spiders."

"Not much you worry about me—or anything else," replied William, good-humoredly. "There! how does that look?" he finished, as he carefully picked his way down the stepladder.

"Fine!—er—only rather warlike, maybe, with the guns and that riotous confusion of knives and scimitars over the chiffonier. But then, maybe you're intending Billy for a soldier; eh?"

"Do you know? I AM getting interested in that boy," beamed William, with some excitement. "What kind of things do you suppose he does like?"

"There's no telling. Maybe he's a sissy chap, and will howl at your guns and spiders. Perhaps he'll prefer autumn leaves and worsted mottoes for decoration."

"Not much he will," contested the other. "No son of Walter Neilson's could be a sissy. Neilson was the best half-back in ten years at Harvard, and he was always in for everything going that was worth while. 'Autumn leaves and worsted mottoes' indeed! Bah!"

"All right; but there's still a dark horse in the case, you know. We mustn't forget—Spunk."

The elder man stirred uneasily.

"Bert, what do you suppose that creature is? You don't think Cyril can be right, and that it's a—monkey?"

"'You never can tell,'" quoted Bertram, merrily. "Of course there ARE other things. If it were you, now, we'd only have to hunt up the special thing you happened to be collecting at the time, and that would be it: a snake, a lizard, a toad, or maybe a butterfly. You know you were always lugging those things home when you were his age."

"Yes, I know," sighed William. "But I can't think it's anything like that," he finished, as he turned away.

There was very little done in the Beacon Street house that day but to "get ready for Billy." In the kitchen Dong Ling cooked. Everywhere else, except in Cyril's domain, Pete dusted and swept and "puttered" to his heart's content. William did not go to the office at all that day, and Bertram did not touch his brushes. Only Cyril attended to his usual work: practising for a coming concert, and correcting the proofs of his new book, "Music in Russia."

At ten minutes before five William, anxious-eyed and nervous, found himself at the North Station. Then, and not till then, did he draw a long breath of relief.

"There! I think everything's ready," he sighed to himself. "At last!"

He wore no pink in his buttonhole. There was no need that he should accede to that silly request, he told himself. He had only to look for a youth of perhaps eighteen years, who would be alone, a little frightened, possibly, and who would have a pink in his buttonhole, and probably a dog on a leash.

As he waited, the man was conscious of a curious warmth at his heart. It was his namesake, Walter Neilson's boy, that he had come to meet; a homesick, lonely orphan who had appealed to him—to him, out of all the world. Long years ago in his own arms there had been laid a tiny bundle of flannel holding a precious little red, puckered face. But in a

Eleanor H. Porter

month's time the little face had turned cold and waxen, and the hopes that the white flannel bundle had carried had died with the baby boy;—and that baby would have been a lad grown by this time, if he had lived—a lad not far from the age of this Billy who was coming to-day, reflected the man. And the warmth in his heart deepened and glowed the more as he stood waiting at the gate for Billy to arrive.

The train from Hampden Falls was late. Not until quite fifteen minutes past five did it roll into the train-shed. Then at once its long line of passengers began to sweep toward the iron gate.

William was just inside the gate now, anxiously scanning every face and form that passed. There were many half-grown lads, but there was not one with a pink in his button-hole until very near the end. Then William saw him—a pleasant-faced, blue-eyed boy in a neat gray suit. With a low cry William started forward; but he saw at once that the gray-clad youth was unmistakably one of a merry family party. He looked to be anything but a lad that was lonely and forlorn.

William hesitated and fell back. This debonair, self-reliant fellow could not be Billy! But as a hasty glance down the line revealed only half a dozen straggling women, and beyond them, no one, William decided that it must be Billy; and taking brave hold of his courage, he hurried after the blue-eyed youth and tapped him on the shoulder.

"Er—aren't you Billy?" he stammered.

The lad stopped and stared. He shook his head slowly.

"No, sir," he said.

"But you must be! Are you sure?"

The boy laughed this time.

"Sorry, sir, but my name is 'Frank'; isn't it, mother?" he added merrily, turning to the lady at his side, who was regarding William very unfavorably through a pair of gold-bowed spectacles.

William did not wait for more. With a stammered apology and a flustered lifting of his hat he backed away.

But where was Billy?

William looked about him in helpless dismay. All around was a wide, empty space. The long aisle to the Hampden Falls train was deserted save for the baggage-men loading the trunks and bags on to their trucks. Nowhere was there any one who seemed forlorn or ill at ease except a pretty girl with a suit-case, and with a covered basket on her arm, who stood just outside the gate, gazing a little nervously about her.

William looked twice at this girl. First, because the splash of color against her brown coat had called his attention to the fact that she was wearing a pink; and secondly because she was very pretty, and her dark eyes carried a peculiarly wistful appeal.

"Too bad Bertram isn't here," thought William. "He'd be sketching that face in no time on his cuff."

The pink had given William almost a pang. He had been so longing to see a pink—though in a different place. He wondered sympathetically if she, too, had come to meet some one who had not appeared. He noticed that she walked away from the gate once or twice, toward the waiting-room, and peered anxiously through the glass doors; but always she came back to the gate as if fearful to be long away from that place. He forgot all about her very soon, for her movements had given him a sudden idea: perhaps Billy was in the waiting-room. How stupid of him not to think of it before! Doubtless they had missed each other in the crowd, and Billy had gone straight to the waiting-room to look for him. And with this thought William hurried away at once, leaving the girl still standing by the gate alone.

He looked everywhere. Systematically he paced up and down between the long rows of seats, looking for a boy with a pink. He even went out upon the street, and gazed anxiously in all directions. It occurred to him after a time that possibly Billy, like himself, had changed his mind at the last moment, and not worn the pink. Perhaps he had forgotten it, or lost it, or even not been able to get it at all. Very bitterly William blamed himself then for disregarding his own part of the suggested plan. If only he had worn the pink himself!—but he had not; and it was useless to repine. In the meantime, where was Billy, he wondered frantically.

CHAPTER VI

THE COMING OF BILLY

After another long search William came back to the train-shed, vaguely hoping that Billy might even then be there. The girl was still standing alone by the gate. There was another train on the track now, and the rush of many feet had swept her a little to one side. She looked frightened now, and almost ready to cry. Still, William noticed that her chin was lifted bravely, and that she was making a stern effort at self-control. He hesitated a moment, then went straight toward her.

"I beg your pardon," he said kindly, lifting his hat, "but I notice that you have been waiting here some time. Perhaps there is something I can do for you."

A rosy color swept to the girl's face. Her eyes lost their frightened appeal, and smiled frankly into his.

"Oh, thank you, sir! There IS something you can do for me, if you will be so kind. You see, I can't leave this place, I'm so afraid he'll come and I'll miss him. But—I think there's some mistake. Could you telephone for me?" Billy Neilson was country-bred, and in Hampden Falls all men served all other men and women, whether they were strangers or not; so to

Billy this was not an extraordinary request to make, in the least.

William Henshaw smiled.

"Certainly; I shall be very glad to telephone for you. Just tell me whom you want, and what you want to say."

"Thank you. If you'll call up Mr. William Henshaw, then, of Beacon Street, please, and tell him Billy's come. I'll wait here."

"Oh, then Billy did come!" cried the man in glad surprise, his face alight. "But where is he? Do YOU know Billy?"

"I should say I did," laughed Billy, with the lightness of a long-lost child who has found a friend. "Why, I am Billy, myself!"

To William Henshaw the world swam dizzily, and went suddenly mad. The floor rose, and the roof fell, while cars and people performed impossible acrobatic feats above, below, and around him. Then, from afar off, he heard his own voice stammer:

"You—are—B-Billy!"

"Yes; and I'll wait here, if you'll just tell him, please. He's expecting me, you know, so it's all right, only perhaps he made a mistake in the time. Maybe you know him, anyhow."

With one mighty effort William Henshaw pulled himself sharply together. He even laughed, and tossed his head in a valiant imitation of Billy herself; but his voice shook.

"Know him!—I should say I did!" he cried. "Why, I am

William Henshaw, myself."

"You!—Uncle William! Why, where's your pink?"

The man's face was already so red it could not get any redder—but it tried to do so.

"Why, er—I—it—er—if you'll just come into the waiting-room a minute, my dear," he stuttered miserably, "I—I'll explain—about that. I shall have to leave you—for a minute," he plunged on frenziedly, as he led the way to a seat; "A—matter of business that I must attend to. I'll be—right back. Wait here, please!" And he almost pushed the girl into a seat and hurried away.

At a safe distance William Henshaw turned and looked back. His knees were shaking, and his fingers had grown cold at their tips. He could see her plainly, as she bent over the basket in her lap. He could see even the pretty curve of her cheek, and of her slender throat when she lifted her head.

And that was Billy—a GIRL!

People near him at that moment saw a flushed-faced, nervous-appearing man throw up his hands with a despairing gesture, roll his eyes heavenward, and then plunge into the nearest telephone booth.

In due time William Henshaw had his brother Bertram at the other end of the wire.

"Bertram!" he called shakily.

"Hullo, Will; that you? What's the matter? You're late! Didn't he come?"

Eleanor H. Porter

"Come!" groaned William. "Good Lord! Bertram—Billy's a GIRL!"

"A wh-what?"

"A girl."

"A GIRL!"

"Yes, yes! Don't stand there repeating what I say in that idiotic fashion, Bertram. Do something—do something!"

"'Do something'!" gasped Bertram. "Great Scott, Will! If you want me to do something, don't knock me silly with a blow like that. Now what did you say?"

"I said that Billy is—a—girl. Can't you get that?" demanded William, despairingly.

"Well, by Jove!" breathed Bertram.

"Come, come, think! What shall we do?"

"Why, bring her home, of course."

"Home—home!" chattered William. "Do you think we five men can bring up a distractingly pretty eighteen-year-old girl with curly cheeks and pink hair?"

"With wha-at?"

"No, no. I mean curly hair and pink cheeks. Bertram, do be sensible," begged the man. "This is serious!"

"Serious! I should say it was! Only fancy what Cy will say! A girl! Holy smoke! Tote her along—I want to see her!"

"But I say we can't keep her there with us, Bertram. Don't you see we can't?"

"Then take her to Kate's, or to—to one of those Young Women's Christian Union things."

"No, no, I can't do that. That's impossible. Don't you understand? She's expecting to go home with me—HOME! I'm her Uncle William."

"Lucky Uncle William!"

"Be still, Bertram!"

"Well, doesn't she know your—mistake?—that you thought she was a boy?"

"Heaven forbid!—I hope not," cried the man, fervently. "I 'most let it out once, but I think she didn't notice it. You see, we—we were both surprised."

"Well, I should say!"

"And, Bertram, I can't turn her out—I can't, I tell you. Only fancy my going to her now and saying: 'If you please, Billy, you can't live at my house, after all. I thought you were a boy, you know!' Great Scott! Bert, if she'd once turned those big brown eyes of hers on you as she has on me, you'd see!"

"I'd be delighted, I'm sure," sung a merry voice across the wires. "Sounds real interesting!"

"Bertram, can't you be serious and help me out?"

"But what CAN we do?"

"I don't know. We'll have to think; but for now, get Kate. Telephone her. Tell her to come right straight over, and that she's got to stay all night."

"All night!"

"Of course! Billy's got to have a chaperon; hasn't she? Now hurry. We shall be up right away."

"Kate's got company."

"Never mind—leave 'em. Tell her she's got to leave 'em. And tell Cyril, of course, what to expect. And, look a-here, you two behave, now. None of your nonsense! Now mind. I'm not going to have this child tormented."

"I won't bat an eyelid—on my word, I won't," chuckled Bertram. "But, oh, I say,—Will!"

"Yes."

"What's Spunk?"

"Eh?—oh—Great Scott! I forgot Spunk. I don't know. She's got a basket. He's in that, I suppose. Anyhow, he can't be any more of a bombshell than his mistress was. Now be quick, and none of your fooling, Bertram. Tell them all—Pete and Dong Ling. Don't forget. I wouldn't have Billy find out for the world! Fix it up with Kate. You'll have to fix it up with her; that's all!" And there came the sharp click of the receiver against the hook.

CHAPTER VII

INTRODUCING SPUNK

In the soft April twilight Cyril was playing a dreamy waltz when Bertram knocked, and pushed open the door.

"Say, old chap, you'll have to quit your mooning this time and sit up and take notice."

"What do you mean?" Cyril stopped playing and turned abruptly.

"I mean that Will has gone crazy, and I think the rest of us are going to follow suit."

Cyril shrugged his shoulders and whirled about on the piano stool. In a moment his fingers had slid once more into the dreamy waltz.

"When you get ready to talk sense, I'll listen," he said coldly.

"Oh, very well; if you really want it broken gently, it's this: Will has met Billy, and Billy is a girl. They're due here now 'most any time."

The music stopped with a crash.

Eleanor H. Porter

"A—GIRL!"

"Yes, a girl. Oh, I've been all through that, and I know how you feel. But as near as I can make out, it's really so. I've had instructions to tell everybody, and I've told. I got Kate on the telephone, and she's coming over. You KNOW what SHE'LL be. Dong Ling is having what I suppose are Chinese hysterics in the kitchen; and Pete is swinging back and forth like a pendulum in the dining-room, moaning 'Good Lord, deliver us!' at every breath. I would suggest that you follow me down-stairs so that we may be decently ready for—whatever comes." And he turned about and stalked out of the room, followed by Cyril, who was too stunned to open his lips.

Kate came first. She was not stunned. She had a great deal to say.

"Really, this is a little the most absurd thing I ever heard of," she fumed. "What in the world does your brother mean?"

That she quite ignored her own relationship to the culprit was not lost on Bertram. He made instant response.

"As near as I can make out," he replied smoothly, "YOUR brother has fallen under the sway of a pair of great dark eyes, two pink cheeks, and an unknown quantity of curly hair, all of which in its entirety is his namesake, is lonesome, and is in need of a home."

"But she can't live—here!"

"Will says she shall."

"But that is utter nonsense," cut in Cyril.

"For once I agree with you, Cyril," laughed Bertram; "but

William doesn't."

"But how can she do it?" demanded Kate.

"Don't know," answered Bertram. "He's established a petticoat propriety in you for a few hours, at least. Meanwhile, he's going to think. At least, he says he is, and that we've got to help him."

"Humph!" snapped Kate. "Well, I can prophesy we sha'n't think alike—so you'd notice it!"

"I know that," nodded Bertram; "and I'm with you and Cyril on this. The whole thing is absurd. The idea of thrusting a silly, eighteen-year-old girl here into our lives in this fashion! But you know what Will is when he's really roused. You might as well try to move a nice good-natured mountain by saying 'please,' as to try to stir him under certain circumstances. Most of the time, I'll own, we can twist him around our little fingers. But not now. You'll see. In the first place, she's the daughter of his dead friend, and she DID write a pathetic little letter. It got to the inside of me, anyhow, when I thought she was a boy."

"A boy! Who wouldn't think she was a boy?" interposed Cyril. "'Billy,' indeed! Can you tell me what for any sane man should have named a girl 'Billy'?"

"For William, your brother, evidently," retorted Bertram, dryly. "Anyhow, he did it, and of course our mistake was a very natural one. The dickens of it is now that we've got to keep it from her, so Will says; and how—hush! here they are," he broke off, as there came the sound of wheels stopping before the house.

There followed the click of a key in the lock and the opening

Eleanor H. Porter

of a heavy door; then, full in the glare of the electric lights stood a plainly nervous man, and a girl with startled, appealing eyes.

"My dear," stammered William, "this is my sister, Kate, Mrs. Hartwell; and here are Cyril and Bertram, whom I've told you of. And of course I don't need to say to them that you are Billy."

It was over. William drew a long breath, and gave an agonized look into his brothers' eyes. Then Billy turned from Mrs. Hartwell and held out a cordial hand to each of the men in turn.

"Oh, you don't know how lovely this is—to me," she cried softly. "And to think that you were willing I should come!" The two younger men caught their breath sharply, and tried not to see each other's eyes. "You look so good—all of you; and I don't believe there's one of you that's got nerves or a heart," she laughed.

Bertram rallied his wits to respond to the challenge.

"No heart, Miss Billy? Now isn't that just a bit hard on us— right at first?"

"Not a mite, if you take it the way I mean it," dimpled Billy. "Hearts that are all right just keep on pumping, and you never know they are there. They aren't worth mentioning. It's the other kind—the kind that flutters at the least noise and jumps at the least bang! And I don't believe any of you mind noises and bangs," she finished merrily, as she handed her hat and coat to Mrs. Hartwell, who was waiting to receive them.

Bertram laughed. Cyril scowled, and occupied himself in

finding a chair. William had already dropped himself wearily on to the sofa near his sister. Billy still continued to talk.

"Now when Spunk and I get to training—oh, and you haven't seen Spunk!" she interrupted herself suddenly. "Why, the introductions aren't half over. Where is he, Uncle William—the basket?"

"I—I put it in—in the hall," mumbled William, starting to rise.

"No, no; I'll get him," cried Billy, hurrying from the room. She returned in a moment, the green covered basket in her hand. "He's been asleep, I guess. He's slept 'most all the way down, anyhow. He's so used to being toted 'round in this basket that he doesn't mind it a bit. I take him everywhere in it at the Falls."

There was an electric pause. Four pairs of startled, questioning, fearful eyes were on the basket while Billy fumbled at the knot of the string. The next moment, with a triumphant flourish, Billy lifted from the basket and placed on the floor a very small gray kitten with a very large pink bow.

"There, ladies and gentlemen, may I present to you, Spunk."

The tiny creature winked and blinked, and balanced for a moment on sleepy legs; then at the uncontrollable shout that burst from Bertram's throat, he faced the man, humped his tiny back, bristled his diminutive tail to almost unbelievable fluffiness, and spit wrathfully.

"And so that is Spunk!" choked Bertram.

"Yes," said Billy. "This is Spunk."

CHAPTER VIII

THE ROOM—AND BILLY

For the first fifteen minutes after Billy's arrival conversation was a fitful thing made up mostly of a merry monologue on the part of Billy herself, interspersed with somewhat dazed replies from one after another of her auditors as she talked to them in turn. No one thought to ask if she cared to go up to her room, and during the entire fifteen minutes Billy sat on the floor with Spunk in her lap. She was still there when the funereal face of Pete appeared in the doorway. Pete's jaw dropped. It was plain that only the sternest self-control enabled him to announce dinner, with anything like dignity. But he managed to stammer out the words, and then turn loftily away. Bertram, who sat near the door, however, saw him raise his hands in horror as he plunged through the hall and down the stairway.

With a motion to Bertram to lead the way with Billy, William frenziedly gripped his sister's arm, and hissed in her ear for all the world like a villain in melodrama:

"Listen! You'll sleep in Bert's room to-night, and Bert will come up-stairs with me. Get Billy to bed as soon as you can after dinner, and then come back down to us. We've got to plan what's got to be done. Sh-h!" And he dragged his sister downstairs.

In the dining-room there was a slight commotion. Billy stood at her chair with Spunk in her arms. Before her Pete was standing, dumbly staring into her eyes. At last he stammered:

"Ma'am?"

"A chair, please, I said, for Spunk, you know. Spunk always sits at the table right next to me."

It was too much for Bertram. He fled chokingly to the hall. William dropped weakly into his own place. Cyril stared as had Pete; but Mrs. Hartwell spoke.

"You don't mean—that that cat—has a chair—at the table!" she gasped.

"Yes; and isn't it cute of him?" beamed Billy, entirely misconstruing the surprise in the lady's voice. "His mother always sat at table with us, and behaved beautifully, too. Of course Spunk is little, and makes mistakes sometimes. But he'll learn. Oh, there's a chair right here," she added, as she spied Bertram's childhood's high-chair, which for long years had stood unused in the corner. "I'll just squeeze it right in here," she finished gleefully, making room for the chair at her side.

When Bertram, a little red of face, but very grave, entered, the dining-room a moment later, he found the family seated with Spunk snugly placed between Billy and a plainly disgusted and dismayed brother, Cyril. The kitten was alert and interested; but he had settled back in his chair, and was looking as absurdly dignified as the flaring pink bow would let him.

Eleanor H. Porter

"Isn't he a dear?" Billy was saying. But Bertram noticed that there was no reply to this question.

It was a peculiar dinner-party. Only Billy did not feel the strain. Even Spunk was not entirely happy—his efforts to investigate the table and its contents were too frequently curbed by his mistress for his unalloyed satisfaction. William, it is true, made a valiant attempt to cause the conversation to be general; but he failed dismally. Kate was sternly silent, while Cyril was openly repellent. Bertram talked, indeed—but Bertram always talked; and very soon he and Billy had things pretty much to themselves—that is, with occasional interruptions caused by Spunk. Spunk had an inquisitive nose or paw for each new dish placed before his mistress; and Billy spent much time admonishing him. Billy said she was training him; that it was wonderful what training would do, and, of course, Spunk WAS little, now.

Dinner was half over when there was a slight diversion created by Spunk's conclusion to get acquainted with the silent man at his left. Cyril, however, did not respond to Spunk's advances. So very evident, indeed, was the man's aversion that Billy turned in amazement.

"Why, Mr. Cyril, don't you see? Spunk is trying to say 'How do you do'?"

"Very likely; but I'm not fond of cats, Miss Billy."

"You're not fond—of—cats!" repeated the girl, as if she could not have heard aright. "Why not?"

Cyril changed his position.

"Why, just because I—I'm not," he retorted lamely. "Isn't there anything that—that you don't like?"

Billy considered.

"Why, not that I know of," she began, after a moment, "only rainy days and—tripe. And Spunk isn't a bit like those."

Bertram chuckled, and even Cyril smiled—though unwillingly.

"All the same," he reiterated, "I don't like cats."

"Oh, I'm so sorry," lamented Billy; and at the grieved hurt in her dark eyes Bertram came promptly to the rescue.

"Never mind, Miss Billy. Cyril is only ONE of us, and there is all the rest of the Strata besides."

"The—what?"

"The Strata. You don't know, of course, but listen, and I'll tell you." And he launched gaily forth into his favorite story.

Billy was duly amused and interested. She laughed and clapped her hands, and when the story was done she clapped them again.

"Oh, what a funny house! And how perfectly lovely that I'm going to live in it," she cried. Then straight at Mrs. Hartwell she hurled a bombshell. "But where is your stratum?" she demanded. "Mr. Bertram didn't mention a thing about you!"

Cyril said a sharp word under his breath. Bertram choked over a cough. Kate threw into William's eyes a look that was at once angry, accusing, and despairing. Then William spoke.

"Er—she—it isn't anywhere, my dear," he stammered; "or

rather, it isn't here. Kate lives up on the Avenue, you see, and is only here for—for a day or two—just now."

"Oh!" murmured Billy. And there was not one in the room at that moment who did not bless Spunk—for Spunk suddenly leaped to the table before him; and in the ensuing confusion his mistress quite forgot to question further concerning Mrs. Hartwell's stratum.

Dinner over, the three men, with their sister and Billy, trailed up-stairs to the drawing-rooms. Billy told them, then, of her life at Hampden Falls. She cried a little at the mention of Aunt Ella; and she portrayed very vividly the lonely life from which she herself had so gladly escaped. She soon had every one laughing, even Cyril, over her stories of the lawyer's home that might have been hers, with its gloom and its hush and its socketed chairs.

As soon as possible, however, Mrs. Hartwell, with a murmured "I know you must be tired, Billy," suggested that the girl go up-stairs to her room. "Come," she added, "I will show you the way."

There was some delay, even then, for Spunk had to be provided with sleeping quarters; and it was not without some hesitation that Billy finally placed the kitten in the reluctant hands of Pete, who had been hastily summoned. Then she turned and followed Mrs. Hartwell up-stairs.

It seemed to the three men in the drawing-room that almost immediately came the piercing shriek, and the excited voice of their sister in expostulation. Without waiting for more they leaped to the stairway and hurried up, two steps at a time.

"For heaven's sake, Kate, what is it?" panted William, who

had been outdistanced by his more agile brothers.

Kate was on her feet, her face the picture of distressed amazement. In the low chair by the window Billy sat where she had flung herself, her hands over her face. Her shoulders were shaking, and from her throat came choking little cries.

"I don't know," quavered Kate. "I haven't the least idea. She was all right till she got up-stairs here, and I turned on the lights. Then she gave one shriek and—you know all I know."

William advanced hurriedly.

"Billy, what is the matter? What are you crying for?" he demanded.

Billy dropped her hands then, and they saw her face. She was not crying. She was laughing. She was laughing so she could scarcely speak.

"Oh, you did, you did!" she gurgled. "I thought you did, and now I know!"

"Did what? What do you mean?" William's usually gentle voice was sharp. Even William's nerves were beginning to feel the strain of the last few hours.

"Thought I was a—b-boy!" choked Billy. "You called me 'he' once in the station—I thought you did; but I wasn't sure—not till I saw this room. But now I know—I know!" And off she went into another hysterical gale of laughter— Billy's nerves, too, were beginning to respond to the excitement of the last few hours.

As to the three men and the woman, they stood silent, helpless, looking into each other's faces with despairing eyes.

Eleanor H. Porter

In a moment Billy was on her feet, fluttering about the room, touching this thing, looking at that. Nothing escaped her.

"I'm to fish—and shoot—and fence!" she crowed. "And, oh! —look at those knives! U-ugh!... And, my! what are these?" she cried, pouncing on the Indian clubs. "And look at the spiders! Dear, dear, I AM glad they're dead, anyhow," she shuddered with a nervous laugh that was almost a sob.

Something in Billy's voice stirred Mrs. Hartwell to sudden action.

"Come, come, this will never do," she protested authoritatively, motioning her brothers to leave the room. "Billy is quite tired out, and needs rest. She mustn't talk another bit tonight."

"Of c-course not," stammered William. And only too glad of an excuse to withdraw from a very embarrassing situation, the three men called back a faltering good-night, and precipitately fled down-stairs.

CHAPTER IX

A FAMILY CONCLAVE

"Well, William," greeted Kate, grimly, when she came into the drawing-room, after putting her charge to bed, "have you had enough, now?"

"'Enough'! What do you mean?"

Kate raised her eyebrows.

"Why, surely, you're not thinking NOW that you can keep this girl here; are you?"

"I don't know why not."

"William!"

"Well, where shall she go? Will you take her?"

"I? Certainly not," declared Kate, with decision. "I'm sure I see no reason why I should."

"No more do I see why William should, either," cut in Cyril.

"Oh, come, what's the use," interposed Bertram. "Let her

stay. She's a nice little thing, I'm sure."

Cyril and Kate turned sharply.

"Bertram!" The cry was a duet of angry amazement. Then Kate added: "It seems that you, too, have come under the sway of dark eyes, pink cheeks, and an unknown quantity of curly hair!"

Bertram laughed.

"Oh, well, she would be nice to—er—paint," he murmured.

"See here, children," demurred William, a little sternly, "all this is wasting time. There is no way out of it. I wouldn't be seen turning that homeless child away now. We must keep her; that's settled. The question is, how shall it be done? We must have some woman friend here to be her companion, of course; but whom shall we get?"

Kate sighed, and looked her dismay. Bertram threw a glance into Cyril's eyes, and made an expressive gesture.

"You see," it seemed to say. "I told you how it would be!"

"Now whom shall we get?" questioned William again. "We must think."

Unattached gentlewomen of suitable age and desirable temper did not prove to be so numerous among the Henshaws' acquaintances, however, as to make the selection of a chaperon very easy. Several were thought of and suggested; but in each case the candidate was found to possess one or more characteristics that made the idea of her presence utterly abhorrent to some one of the brothers. At last William expostulated:

"See here, boys, we aren't any nearer a settlement than we were in the first place. There isn't any woman, of course, who would exactly suit all of us; and so we shall just have to be willing to take some one who doesn't."

"The trouble is," explained Bertram, airily, "we want some one who will be invisible to every one except the world and Billy, and who will be inaudible always."

"I don't know but you are right," sighed William. "But suppose we settle on Aunt Hannah. She seems to be the least objectionable of the lot, and I think she'd come. She's alone in the world, and I believe the comfortable roominess of this house would be very grateful to her after the inconvenience of her stuffy little room over at the Back Bay."

"You bet it would!" murmured Bertram, feelingly; but William did not appear to hear him.

"She's amiable, fairly sensible, and always a lady," he went on; "and to-morrow morning I believe I'll run over and see if she can't come right away."

"And may I ask which—er—stratum she—they—will occupy?" smiled Bertram.

"You may ask, but I'm afraid you won't find out very soon," retorted William, dryly, "if we take as long to decide that matter as we have the rest of it."

"Er—Cyril has the most—UNOCCUPIED space," volunteered Bertram, cheerfully.

"Indeed!" retaliated Cyril. "Suppose you let me speak for myself! Of course, so far as truck is concerned, I'm not in it with you and Will. But as for the USE I put my rooms to—!

Besides, I already have Pete there, and would have Dong Ling probably, if he slept here. However, if you want any of my rooms, don't let my petty wants and wishes interfere—"

"No, no," interrupted William, in quick conciliation. "We don't want your rooms, Cyril. Aunt Hannah abhors stairs. Of course I might move, I suppose. My rooms are one flight less; but if I only didn't have so many things!"

"Oh, you men!" shrugged Kate, wearily. "Why don't you ask my opinion sometimes? It seems to me that in this case a woman's wit might be of some help!"

"All right, go ahead!" nodded William.

Kate leaned forward eagerly—Kate loved to "manage."

"Go easy, now," cautioned Bertram, warily. "You know a strata, even one as solid as ours, won't stand too much of an earthquake!"

"It isn't an earthquake at all," sniffed Kate. "It's a very sensible move all around. Here are these two great drawing-rooms, the library, and the little reception-room across the hall, and not one of them is ever used but this. Of course the women wouldn't like to sleep down here, but why don't you, Bertram, take the back drawing-room, the library, and the little reception-room for yours, and leave the whole of the second floor for Billy and Aunt Hannah?"

"Good for you, Kate," cried Bertram, appreciatively. "You've hit it square on the head, and we'll do it. I'll move to-morrow. The light down here is just as good as it is up-stairs—if you let it in!"

"Thank you, Bertram, and you, too, Kate," breathed William,

fervently. "Now, if you don't mind, I believe I'll go to bed. I am tired!"

Eleanor H. Porter

CHAPTER X

AUNT HANNAH

As soon as possible after breakfast William went to see Aunt Hannah.

Hannah Stetson was not really William's aunt, though she had been called Aunt Hannah for years. She was the widow of a distant cousin, and she lived in a snug little room in a Back Bay boarding-house. She was a slender, white-haired woman with kind blue eyes, and a lovable smile. Her cheeks were still faintly pink, and her fine silver-white hair broke into little kinks and curls about her ears. According to Bertram she always made one think of "lavender and old lace."

She welcomed William cordially this morning, though with faint surprise in her eyes.

"Yes, I know I'm an early caller, and an unexpected one," began William, hurriedly. "And I shall have to plunge straight into the matter, too, for there isn't time to preamble. I've taken an eighteen-year-old girl to bring up, Aunt Hannah, and I want you to come down and live with us to chaperon her."

"My grief and conscience, WILLIAM!" gasped the little woman, agitatedly.

"Yes, yes, I know, Aunt Hannah, everything you would say if you could. But please skip the hysterics. We've all had them, and Kate has already used every possible adjective that you could think up. Now it's just this." And he hurriedly gave Mrs. Stetson a full account of the case, and told her plainly what he hoped and expected that she would do for him.

"Why, yes, of course—I'll come," acquiesced the lady, a little breathlessly, "if—if you are sure you're going to—keep her."

"Good! And remember I said 'now,' please—that I wanted you to come right away, to-day. Of course Kate can't stay. Just get in half a dozen women to help you pack, and come."

"Half a dozen women in that little room, William—impossible!"

"Well, I only meant to get enough so you could come right off this morning."

"But I don't need them, William. There are only my clothes and books, and such things. You know it is a FURNISHED room."

"All right, all right, Aunt Hannah. I wanted to make sure you hurried, that's all. You see, I don't want Billy to suspect just how much she's upsetting us. I've asked Kate to take her over to her house for the day, while Bertram is moving down-stairs, and while we're getting you settled. I—I think you'll like it there, Aunt Hannah," added William, anxiously. "Of course Billy's got Spunk, but—" he hesitated, and smiled a little.

"Got what?" faltered the other.

"Spunk. Oh, I don't mean THAT kind," laughed William, in answer to the dismayed expression on his aunt's face. "Spunk is a cat."

"A cat!—but such a name, William! I—I think we'll change that."

"Eh? Oh, you do," murmured William, with a curious smile. "Very well; be that as it may. Anyhow, you're coming, and we shall want you all settled by dinner time," he finished, as he picked up his hat to go.

With Kate, Billy spent the long day very contentedly in Kate's beautiful Commonwealth Avenue home. The two boys, Paul, twelve years old, and Egbert, eight, were a little shy, it is true, and not really of much use as companions; but there was a little Kate, four years old, who proved to be wonderfully entertaining.

Billy was not much used to children, and she found this four-year-old atom of humanity to be a great source of interest and amusement. She even told Mrs. Hartwell at parting that little Kate was almost as nice as Spunk—which remark, oddly enough, did not appear to please Mrs. Hartwell to the extent that Billy thought that it would.

At the Beacon Street house Billy was presented at once to Mrs. Stetson.

"And you are to call me 'Aunt Hannah,' my dear," said the little woman, graciously, "just as the boys do."

"Thank you," dimpled Billy, "and you don't know, Aunt Hannah, how good it seems to me to come into so many relatives, all at once!"

Upon going up-stairs Billy found her room somewhat changed. It was far less warlike, and the case of spiders had been taken away.

"And this will be your stratum, you know," announced Bertram from the stairway, "yours and Aunt Hannah's. You're to have this whole floor. Will and Cyril are above, and I'm down-stairs."

"You are? Why, I thought you—were—here." Billy's face was puzzled.

"Here? Oh, well, I did have—some things here," he retorted airily; "but I took them all away to-day. You see, my stratum is down-stairs, and it doesn't do to mix the layers. By the way, you haven't been up-stairs yet; have you? Come on, and I'll show you—and you, too, Aunt Hannah."

Billy clapped her hands; but Aunt Hannah shook her head.

"I'll leave that for younger feet than mine," she said; adding whimsically: "It's best sometimes that one doesn't try to step too far off one's own level, you know."

"All right," laughed the man. "Come on, Miss Billy."

On the door at the head of the stairs he tapped twice, lightly.

"Well, Pete," called Cyril's voice, none too cordially.

"Pete, indeed!" scoffed Bertram. "You've got company, young man. Open the door. Miss Billy is viewing the Strata."

The bare floor echoed to a quick tread, then the door opened and Cyril faced them with a forced smile on his lips.

"Come in—though I fear there will be little—to see," he said.

Bertram assumed a pompous attitude.

"Ladies and gentlemen; you behold here the lion in his lair."

"Be still, Bertram," ordered Cyril.

"He is a lion, really," confided Bertram, in a lower voice; "but as he prefers it, we'll just call him 'the Musical Man.'"

"I should think I was some sort of music-box that turned with a crank," bristled Cyril.

Bertram grinned.

"A—CRANK, did you say? Well, even I wouldn't have quite dared to say that, you know!"

With an impatient gesture Cyril turned on his heel. Bertram fell once more into his pompous attitude.

"Before you is the Man's workshop," he orated. "At your right you see his instruments of tor—I mean, his instruments: a piano, flute, etc. At your left is the desk with its pens, paper, erasers, ink and postage stamps. I mention these because there are—er—so few things to mention here. Beyond, through the open door, one may catch glimpses of still other rooms; but they hold even less than this one holds. Tradition doth assert, however, that in one is a couch-bed, and in another, two chairs."

Billy listened silently. Her eyes were questioning. She was not quite sure how to take Bertram's words; and the bare rooms and their stern-faced master filled her with a vague pity. But the pause that followed Bertram's nonsense seemed to be waiting for her to fill it.

"Oh, I should like to hear you—play, Mr. Cyril," she stammered. Then, gathering courage. "CAN you play 'The Maiden's Prayer'?"

Bertram gave a cough, a spasmodic cough that sent him, red-faced, out into the hall. From there he called:

"Can't stop for the animals to perform, Miss Billy. It's 'most dinner time, and we've got lots to see yet."

"All right; but—sometime," nodded Billy over her shoulder to Cyril as she turned away. "I just love that 'Maiden's Prayer'!"

"Now this is William's stratum," announced Bertram at the foot of the stairs. "You will perceive that there is no knocking here; William's doors are always open."

"By all means! Come in—come in," called William's cheery voice.

"Oh, my, what a lot of things!" exclaimed Billy. "My—my—what a lot of things! How Spunk will like this room!"

Bertram chuckled; then he made a great display of drawing a long breath.

"In the short time at our disposal," he began loftily, "it will be impossible to point out each particular article and give its history from the beginning; but somewhere you will find four round white stones, which—"

"Er—yes, we know all about those white stones," interrupted William, "and you'll please let me talk about my own things myself!" And he beamed benevolently on the wondering-eyed girl at Bertram's side.

"But there are so many!" breathed Billy.

"All the more chance then," smiled William, "that some-where among them you'll find something to interest you. Now these Chinese ceramics, and these bronzes—maybe you'd like those," he suggested. And with a resigned sigh and an exaggerated air of submission, Bertram stepped back and gave way to his brother.

"And there are these miniatures, and these Japanese porce-lains. Or perhaps you'd like stamps, or theatre programs better," William finished anxiously.

Billy did not reply. She was turning round and round, her eyes wide and amazed. Suddenly she pounced on a beauty-fully decorated teapot, and held it up in admiring hands.

"Oh, what a pretty teapot! And what a cute little plate it sets in!" she cried.

The collector fairly bubbled over with joy.

"That's a Lowestoft—a real Lowestoft!" he crowed. "Not that hard-paste stuff from the Orient that's CALLED Lowestoft, but the real thing—English, you know. And that's the tray that goes with it, too. Wonderful—how I got them both! You know they 'most always get separated. I paid a cool hundred for them, anyhow."

"A hundred dollars for a teapot!" gasped Billy.

"Yes; and here's a nice little piece of lustre-ware. Pretty—isn't it? And there's a fine bit of black basalt. And—"

"Er—Will," interposed Bertram, meekly.

"Oh, and here's a Castleford," cried William, paying no attention to the interruption. "Marked, too; see? 'D. D. & Co., Castleford.' You know there isn't much of that ware marked. This is a beauty, too, I think. You see this pitted surface—they made that with tiny little points set into the inner side of the mold. The design stands out fine on this. It's one of the best I ever saw. And, oh—"

"Er—William," interposed Bertram again, a little louder this time. "May I just say—"

"And did you notice this 'Old Blue'?" hurried on William, eagerly. "Lid sets down in, you see—that's older than the kind where it sets over the top. Now here's one—"

"William," almost shouted Bertram, "DINNER IS READY! Pete has sounded the gong twice already!"

"Eh? Oh, sure enough—sure enough," acknowledged William, with a regretful glance at his treasures. "Well, we must go, we must go."

"But I haven't seen your stratum at all," demurred Billy to her guide, as they went down the stairway.

"Then there's something left for to-morrow," promised Bertram; "but you must remember, I haven't got any beautiful 'Old Blues' and 'black basalts,' to say nothing of stamps and baggage tags. But I'll make you some tea—some real tea—and that's more than William has done, with all his hundred and one teapots!"

Eleanor H. Porter

CHAPTER XI

BERTRAM HAS VISITORS

Spunk did not change his name; but that was perhaps the only thing that did not meet with some sort of change during the weeks that immediately followed Billy's arrival. Given a house, five men, and an ironbound routine of life, and it is scarcely necessary to say that the advent of a somewhat fussy elderly woman, an impulsive young girl, and a very-much-alive small cat will make some difference. As to Spunk's name—it was not Mrs. Stetson's fault that even that was left undisturbed.

Mrs. Stetson early became acquainted with Spunk. She was introduced to him, indeed, on the night of her arrival— though fortunately not at table: William had seen to it that Spunk did not appear at dinner, though to accomplish this the man had been obliged to face the amazed and grieved indignation of the kitten's mistress.

"But I don't see how any one CAN object to a nice clean little cat at the table," Billy had remonstrated tearfully.

"I know; but—er—they do, sometimes," William had stammered; "and this is one of the times. Aunt Hannah would never stand for it—never!"

"Oh, but she doesn't know Spunk," Billy had observed then, hopefully. "You just wait until she knows him."

Mrs. Stetson began to "know" Spunk the next day. The immediate source of her knowledge was the discovery that Spunk had found her ball of black knitting yarn, and had delightedly captured it. Not that he was content to let it remain where it was—indeed, no. He rolled it down the stairs, batted it through the hall to the drawing-room, and then proceeded to 'chasse' with it in and out among the legs of various chairs and tables, ending in one grand whirl that wound the yarn round and round his small body, and keeled him over half upon his back. There he blissfully went to sleep.

Billy found him after a gleeful following of the slender woollen trail. Mrs. Stetson was with her—but she was not gleeful.

"Oh, Aunt Hannah, Aunt Hannah," gurgled Billy, "isn't he just too cute for anything?"

Aunt Hannah shook her head.

"I must confess I don't see it," she declared. "My dear, just look at that hopeless snarl!"

"Oh, but it isn't hopeless at all," laughed Billy. "It's like one of those strings they unwind at parties with a present at the end of it. And Spunk is the present," she added, when she had extricated the small gray cat. "And you shall hold him," she finished, graciously entrusting the sleepy kitten to Mrs. Stetson's unwilling arms.

"But, I—it—I can't—Billy! I don't like that name," blurted out the indignant little lady with as much warmth as she ever

Eleanor H. Porter

allowed herself to show. "It must be changed to—to 'Thomas.'"

"Changed? Spunk's name changed?" demanded Billy, in a horrified voice. "Why, Aunt Hannah, it can't be changed; it's HIS, you know." Then she laughed merrily. "'Thomas,' indeed! Why, you old dear!—just suppose I should ask YOU to change your name! Now *I* like 'Helen Clarabella' lots better than 'Hannah,' but I'm not going to ask you to change that—and I'm going to love you just as well, even if you are 'Hannah'—see if I don't! And you'll love Spunk, too, I'm sure you will. Now watch me find the end of this snarl!" And she danced over to the dumbfounded little lady in the big chair, gave her an affectionate kiss, and then attacked the tangled mass of black with skilful fingers.

"But, I—you—oh, my grief and conscience!" finished the little woman whose name was not Helen Clarabella.—"Oh, my grief and conscience," according to Bertram, was Aunt Hannah's deadliest swear-word.

In Aunt Hannah's black silk lap Spunk stretched luxuriously, and blinked sleepy eyes; then with a long purr of content he curled himself for another nap—still Spunk.

It was some time after luncheon that day that Bertram heard a knock at his studio door. Bertram was busy. His particular pet "Face of a Girl" was to be submitted soon to the judges of a forthcoming Art Exhibition, and it was not yet finished. He was trying to make up now for the many hours lost during the last few days; and even Bertram, at times, did not like interruptions. His model had gone, but he was still working rapidly when the knock came. His tone was not quite cordial when he answered.

"Well?"

"It's I—Spunk and I. May we come in?" called a confident voice.

Bertram said a sharp word behind his teeth—but he opened the door.

"Of course! I was—painting," he announced.

"How lovely! And I'll watch you. Oh, my—what a pretty room!"

"I'm glad you like it."

"Indeed I do; I like it ever so much. I shall stay here lots, I know."

"Oh, you—will!" For once even Bertram's ready tongue failed to find fitting response.

"Yes. Now paint. I want to see you. Aunt Hannah has gone out anyway, and I'm lonesome. I think I'll stay."

"But I can't—that is, I'm not used to spectators."

"Of course you aren't, you poor old lonesomeness! But it isn't going to be that way, any more, you know, now that I've come. I sha'n't let you be lonesome."

"I could swear to that," declared the man, with sudden fervor; and for Billy's peace of mind it was just as well, perhaps, that she did not know the exact source of that fervency.

"Now paint," commanded Billy again.

Because he did not know what else to do, Bertram picked up

a brush; but he did not paint. The first stroke of his brush against the canvas was to Spunk a challenge; and Spunk never refused a challenge. With a bound he was on Bertram's knee, gleeful paw outstretched, batting at the end of the brush.

"Tut, tut—no, no—naughty Spunk! Say, but wasn't that cute?" chuckled Billy. "Do it again!"

The artist gave an exasperated sigh.

"My dear girl," he protested, "cruel as it may seem to you, this picture is not a kindergarten game for the edification of small cats. I must politely ask Spunk to desist."

"But he won't!" laughed Billy. "Never mind; we will take it some day when he's asleep. Let's not paint any more, any-how. I've come to see your rooms." And she sprang blithely to her feet. "Dear, dear, what a lot of faces!—and all girls, too! How funny! Why don't you paint other things? Still, they are rather nice."

"Thank you," accepted Bertram; dryly.

Bertram did not paint any more that afternoon. Billy found much to interest her, and she asked numberless questions. She was greatly excited when she understood the full significance of the omnipresent "Face of a Girl"; and she graciously offered to pose herself for the artist. She spent, indeed, quite half an hour turning her head from side to side, and demanding "Now how's that?—and that?" Tiring at last of this, she suggested Spunk as a substitute, remarking that, after all, cats—pretty cats like Spunk—were even nicer to paint than girls.

She rescued Spunk then from the paint-box where he had

been holding high carnival with Bertram's tubes of paint, and demanded if Bertram ever saw a more delightful, more entrancing, more altogether-to-be-desired model. She was so artless, so merry, so frankly charmed with it all that Bertram could not find it in his heart to be angry, notwithstanding his annoyance. But when at four o'clock, she took herself and her cat cheerily up-stairs, he lifted his hands in despair.

"Great Scott!" he groaned. "If this is a sample of what's coming—I'm GOING, that's all!"

Eleanor H. Porter

CHAPTER XII

CYRIL TAKES HIS TURN

Billy had been a member of the Beacon Street household a week before she repeated her visit to Cyril at the top of the house. This time Bertram was not with her. She went alone. Even Spunk was left behind—Billy remembered her prospective host's aversion to cats.

Billy did not feel that she knew Cyril very well. She had tried several times to chat with him; but she had made so little headway, that she finally came to the conclusion— privately expressed to Bertram—that Mr. Cyril was bashful. Bertram had only laughed. He had laughed the harder because at that moment he could hear Cyril pounding out his angry annoyance on the piano upstairs—Cyril had just escaped from one of Billy's most determined "attempts," and Bertram knew it. Bertram's laugh had puzzled Billy—and it had not quite pleased her. Hence to-day she did not tell him of her plan to go up-stairs and see what she could do herself, alone, to combat this "foolish bashfulness" on the part of Mr. Cyril Henshaw.

In spite of her bravery, Billy waited quite one whole minute at the top of the stairs before she had the courage to knock at Cyril's door.

The door was opened at once.

"Why—Billy!" cried the man in surprise.

"Yes, it's Billy. I—I came up to—to get acquainted," she smiled winningly.

"Why, er—you are very kind. Will you—come in?"

"Thank you; yes. You see, I didn't bring Spunk. I—remembered."

Cyril bowed gravely.

"You are very kind—again," he said.

Billy fidgeted in her chair. To her mind she was not "getting on" at all. She determined on a bold stroke.

"You see, I thought if—if I should come up here, where there wouldn't be so many around, we might get acquainted," she confided; "then I would get to like you just as well as I do the others."

At the odd look that came into the man's face, the girl realized suddenly what she had said. Her cheeks flushed a confused red.

"Oh, dear! That is, I mean—I like you, of course," she floundered miserably; then she broke off with a frank laugh. "There! you see I never could get out of anything. I might as well own right up. I DON'T like you as well as I do Uncle William and Mr. Bertram. So there!"

Cyril laughed. For the first time since he had seen Billy, something that was very like interest came into his eyes.

"Oh, you don't," he retorted. "Now that is—er—very UNkind of you."

Billy shook her head.

"You don't say that as if you meant it," she accused him, her eyes gravely studying his face. "Now I'M in earnest. *I* really want to like YOU!"

"Thank you. Then perhaps you won't mind telling me why you don't like me," he suggested.

Again Billy flushed.

"Why, I—I just don't; that's all," she faltered. Then she cried aggrievedly: "There, now! you've made me be impolite; and I didn't mean to be, truly."

"Of course not," assented the man; "and it wasn't impolite, because I asked you for the information, you know. I may conclude then," he went on with an odd twinkle in his eyes, "that I am merely classed with tripe and rainy days."

"With—wha-at?"

"Tripe and rainy days. Those are the only things, if I remember rightly, that you don't like."

The girl stared; then she chuckled.

"There! I knew I'd like you better if you'd only SAY something," she beamed. "But let's not talk any more about that. Play to me; won't you? You know you promised me 'The Maiden's Prayer.'"

Cyril stiffened.

"Pardon me, but you must be mistaken," he replied coldly. "I do not play 'The Maiden's Prayer.'"

"Oh, what a shame! And I do so love it! But you play other things; I've heard you a little, and Mr. Bertram says you do—in concerts and things."

"Does he?" murmured Cyril, with a slight lifting of his eyebrows.

"There! Now off you go again all silent and horrid!" chaffed Billy. "What have I said now? Mr. Cyril—do you know what I think? I believe you've got NERVES!" Billy's voice was so tragic that the man could but laugh.

"Perhaps I have, Miss Billy."

"Like Miss Letty's?"

"I'm not acquainted with the lady."

"Gee! wouldn't you two make a pair!" chuckled Billy unexpectedly. "No; but, really, I mean—do you want people to walk on tiptoe and speak in whispers?"

"Sometimes, perhaps."

The girl sprang to her feet—but she sighed.

"Then I'm going. This might be one of the times, you know." She hesitated, then walked to the piano. "My, wouldn't I like to play on that!" she breathed.

Cyril shuddered. Cyril could imagine what Billy would play—and Cyril did not like "rag-time," nor "The Storm."

"Oh, do you play?" he asked constrainedly.

Billy shook her head.

"Not much. Only little bits of things, you know," she said wistfully, as she turned toward the door.

For some minutes after she had gone, Cyril stood where she had left him, his eyes moody and troubled.

"I suppose I might have played—something," he muttered at last; "but—'The Maiden's Prayer'!—good heavens!"

Billy was a little shy with Cyril when he came down to dinner that night. For the next few days, indeed, she held herself very obviously aloof from him. Cyril caught himself wondering once if she were afraid of his "nerves." He did not try to find out, however; he was too emphatically content that of her own accord she seemed to be leaving him in peace.

It must have been a week after Billy's visit to the top of the house that Cyril stopped his playing very abruptly one day, and opened his door to go down-stairs. At the first step he started back in amazement.

"Why, Billy!" he ejaculated.

The girl was sitting very near the top of the stairway. At his appearance she got to her feet shamefacedly.

"Why, Billy, what in the world are you doing there?"

"Listening."

"Listening!"

"Yes. Do you mind?"

The man did not answer. He was too surprised to find words at once, and he was trying to recollect what he had been playing.

"You see, listening to music this way isn't like listening to—to talking," hurried on Billy, feverishly. "It isn't sneaking like that; is it?"

"Why—no."

"And you don't mind?"

"Why, surely, I ought not to mind—that," he admitted.

"Then I can keep right on as I have done. Thank you," sighed Billy, in relief.

"Keep right on! Have you been here before?"

"Why, yes, lots of days. And, say, Mr. Cyril, what is that—that thing that's all chords with big bass notes that keep saying something so fine and splendid that it marches on and on, getting bigger and grander, just as if there couldn't anything stop it, until it all ends in one great burst of triumph? Mr. Cyril, what is that?"

"Why, Billy!"—the interest this time in the man's face was not faint—"I wish I might make others catch my meaning as I have evidently made you do it! That's something of my own—that I'm writing, you understand; and I've tried to say—just what you say you heard."

"And I did hear it—I did! Oh, won't you play it, please, with the door open?"

"I can't, Billy. I'm sorry, indeed I am. But I've an appointment, and I'm late now. You shall hear it, though, I promise you, and with the door wide open," continued the man, as, with a murmured apology, he passed the girl and hurried down the stairs.

Billy waited until she heard the outer hall door shut; then very softly she crept through Cyril's open doorway, and crossed the room to the piano.

CHAPTER XIII

A SURPRISE ALL AROUND

May came, and with it warm sunny days. There was a little balcony at the rear of the second floor, and on this Mrs. Stetson and Billy sat many a morning and sewed. There were occupations that Billy liked better than sewing; but she was dutiful, and she was really fond of Aunt Hannah; so she accepted as gracefully as possible that good lady's dictum that a woman who could not sew, and sew well, was no lady at all.

One of the things that Billy liked to do so much better than to sew was to play on Cyril's piano. She was very careful, however, that Mr. Cyril himself did not find this out. Cyril was frequently gone from the house, and almost as frequently Aunt Hannah took naps. At such times it was very easy to slip up-stairs to Cyril's rooms, and once at the piano, Billy forgot everything else.

One day, however, the inevitable happened: Cyril came home unexpectedly. The man heard the piano from William's floor, and with a surprised ejaculation he hurried upstairs two steps at a time. At the door he stopped in amazement.

Billy was at the piano, but she was not playing "rag-time,"

"The Storm," nor yet "The Maiden's Prayer." There was no music before her, but under her fingers "big bass notes" very much like Cyril's own, were marching on and on to victory. Billy's face was rapturously intent and happy.

"By Jove—Billy!" gasped the man.

Billy leaped to her feet and whirled around guiltily.

"Oh, Mr. Cyril—I'm so sorry!"

"Sorry!—and you play like that!"

"No, no; I'm not sorry I played. It's because you—found me."

Billy's cheeks were a shamed red, but her eyes were defiantly brilliant, and her chin was at a rebellious tilt. "I wasn't doing any—harm; not if you weren't here—with your NERVES!"

The man laughed and came slowly into the room.

"Billy, who taught you to play?"

"No one. I can't play. I can only pick out little bits of things in C."

"But you do play. I just heard you."

Billy shrugged her shoulders.

"That was nothing. It was only what I had heard. I was trying to make it sound like—yours."

"And, by George! you succeeded," muttered Cyril under his breath; then aloud he asked: "Didn't you ever study music?"

Billy's eyes dimmed.

"No. That was the only thing Aunt Ella and I didn't think alike about. She had an old square piano, all tin-panny and thin, you know. I played some on it, and wanted to take lessons; but I didn't want to practise on that. I wanted a new one. That's what she wouldn't do—get me a new piano, or let me do it. She said SHE practised on that piano, and that it was quite good enough for me, especially to learn on. I—I'm afraid I got stuffy. I hated that piano so! But I was almost ready to give in when—when Aunt Ella died."

"And all you play then is just by ear?"

"By—ear? I suppose so—if you mean what I hear. Easy things I can play quick, but—but those chords ARE hard; they skip around so!"

Cyril smiled oddly.

"I should say so," he agreed. "But perhaps there is something else that I play—that you like. Is there?"

"Oh, yes. Now there's that little thing that swings and sways like this," cried Billy, dropping herself on to the piano stool and whisking about. Billy was not afraid now, nor defiant. She was only eager and happy again. In a moment a dreamy waltz fell upon Cyril's ears—a waltz that he often played himself. It was not played correctly, it is true. There were notes, and sometimes whole measures, that were very different from the printed music. But the tune, the rhythm, and the spirit were there.

"And there's this," said Billy; "and this," she went on, sliding into one little strain after another—all of which were recognized by the amazed man at her side.

"Billy," he cried, when she had finished and whirled upon him again, "Billy, would you like to learn to play—really play from notes?"

"Oh, wouldn't I!"

"Then you shall! We'll have a piano tomorrow in your rooms for you to practise on. And—I'll teach you myself."

"Oh, thank you, Mr. Cyril—you don't know how I thank you!" exulted Billy, as she danced from the room to tell Aunt Hannah of this great and good thing that had come into her life.

To Billy, this promise of Cyril's to be her teacher was very kind, very delightful; but it was not in the least a thing at which to marvel. To Bertram, however, it most certainly was.

"Well, guess what's happened," he said to William that night, after he had heard the news. "I'll believe anything now—anything: that you'll raffle off your collection of teapots at the next church fair, or that I shall go to Egypt as a 'Cooky' guide. Listen; Cyril is going to give piano lessons to Billy!—CYRIL!"

CHAPTER XIV

AUNT HANNAH SPEAKS HER MIND

Bertram said that the Strata was not a strata any longer. He declared that between them, Billy and Spunk had caused such an upheaval that there was no telling where one stratum left off and another began. What Billy had not attended to, Spunk had, he said.

"You see, it's like this," he explained to an amused friend one day. "Billy is taking piano lessons of Cyril, and she is posing for one of my heads. Naturally, then, such feminine belongings as fancy-work, thread, thimbles, and hairpins are due to show up at any time either in Cyril's apartments or mine—to say nothing of William's; and she's in William's lots—to look for Spunk, if for no other purpose.

"You must know that Spunk likes William's floor the best of the bunch, there are so many delightful things to play with. Not that Spunk stays there—dear me, no. He's a sociable little chap, and his usual course is to pounce on a shelf, knock off some object that tickles his fancy, then lug it in his mouth to—well, anywhere that he happens to feel like going. Cyril has found him up-stairs with a small miniature, battered and chewed almost beyond recognition. And Aunt Hannah nearly had a fit one day when he appeared in her room with an enormous hard-shelled black bug—dead, of course—that he had fished from a case that Pete had left open. As for me, I can swear that the little round white stone he was playing with in my part of the house was one of William's Collection Number One.

"And that isn't all," Bertram continued. "Billy brings her music down to show to me, and lugs my heads all over the rest of the house to show to other folks. And there is always everywhere a knit shawl, for Aunt Hannah is sure to feel a draught, and Billy keeps shawls handy. So there you are! We certainly aren't a strata any longer," he finished.

Billy was, indeed, very much at home in the Beacon Street house—too much so, Aunt Hannah thought. Aunt Hannah was, in fact, seriously disturbed. To William one evening, late in May, she spoke her mind.

"William, what are you going to do with Billy?" she asked abruptly.

"Do with her? What do you mean?" returned William with the contented smile that was so often on his lips these days. "This is Billy's home."

"That's the worst of it," sighed the woman, with a shake of her head.

"The worst of it! Aunt Hannah, what do you mean? Don't you like Billy?"

"Yes, yes, William, of course I like Billy. I love her! Who could help it? That's not what I mean. It's of Billy I'm thinking, and of the rest of you. She can't stay here like this. She must go away, to school, or—or somewhere."

"And she's going in September," replied the man. "She'll go to preparatory school first, and to college, probably."

"Yes, but now—right away. She ought to go—somewhere."

"Why, yes, for the summer, of course. But those plans aren't completed yet. Billy and I were talking of it last evening. You know the boys are always away more or less, but I seldom go until August, and we let Pete and Dong Ling off then for a month and close the house. I told Billy I'd send you and her anywhere she liked for the whole summer, but she says no. She prefers to stay here with me. But I don't quite fancy that idea—through all the hot June and July—so I don't know but I'll get a cottage somewhere near at one of the beaches, where I can run back and forth night and morning. Of course, in that case, we take Pete and Dong Ling with us and close the house right away. I fear Cyril would not fancy it much; but, after all, he and Bertram would be off more or less. They always are in the summer."

"But, William, you haven't yet got my idea at all," demurred Aunt Hannah, with a discouraged shake of her head. "It's away!—away from all this—from you—that I want to get Billy."

"Away! Away from me," cried the man, with an odd intonation of terror, as he started forward in his chair. "Why, Aunt Hannah, what are you talking about?"

"About Billy. This is no place in which to bring up a young girl—a young girl who has not one shred of relationship to excuse it."

"But she is my namesake, and quite alone in the world, Aunt Hannah; quite alone—poor child!"

"My dear William, that is exactly it—she is a child, and yet she is not. That's where the trouble lies."

"What do you mean?"

"William, Billy has been brought up in a little country town with a spinster aunt and a whole good-natured, tolerant village for company. Well, she has accepted you and your entire household, even down to Dong Ling, on the same basis."

"Well, I'm sure I'm glad," asserted the man with genial warmth. "It's good for us to have her here. It's good for the boys. She's already livened Cyril up and toned Bertram down. I may as well confess, Aunt Hannah, that I've been more than a little disturbed about Bertram of late. I don't like that Bob Seaver that he is so fond of; and some other fellows, too, that have been coming here altogether too much during the last year. Bertram says they're only a little 'Bohemian' in their tastes. And to me that's the worst of it, for Bertram himself is quite too much inclined that way."

"Exactly, William. And that only goes to prove what I said before. Bertram is not a spinster aunt, and neither are any of the rest of you. But Billy takes you that way."

"Takes us that way—as spinster aunts!"

"Yes. She makes herself as free in this house as she was in her Aunt Ella's at Hampden Falls. She flies up to Cyril's rooms half a dozen times a day with some question about her lessons; and I don't know how long she'd sit at his feet and adoringly listen to his playing if he didn't sometimes get out of patience and tell her to go and practise herself. She makes nothing of tripping into Bertram's studio at all hours of the day; and he's sketched her head at every conceivable angle—

which certainly doesn't tend to make Billy modest or retiring. As to you—you know how much she's in your rooms, spending evening after evening fussing over your collections."

"I know; but we're—we're sorting them and making a catalogue," defended the man, anxiously. "Besides, I—I like to have her there. She doesn't bother me a bit."

"No; I know she doesn't," replied Aunt Hannah, with a curious inflection. "But don't you see, William, that all this isn't going to quite do? Billy's too young—and too old."

"Come, come, Aunt Hannah, is that exactly logical?"

"It's true, at least."

"But, after all, where's the harm? Don't you think that you are just a little bit too—fastidious? Billy's nothing but a carefree child."

"It's the 'free' part that I object to, William. She has taken every one of you into intimate companionship—even Pete and Dong Ling."

"Pete and Dong Ling!"

"Yes." Mrs. Stetson's chin came up, and her nostrils dilated a little. "Billy went to Pete the other day to have him button her shirt-waist up in the back; and yesterday I found her down-stairs in the kitchen instructing Dong Ling how to make chocolate fudge!"

William fell back in his chair.

"Well, well," he muttered, "well, well! She is a child, and no mistake!" He paused, his brows drawn into a troubled frown.

Eleanor H. Porter

"But, Aunt Hannah, what CAN I do? Of course you could talk to her, but—I don't seem to quite like that idea."

"My grief and conscience—no, no! That isn't what is needed at all. It would only serve to make her self-conscious; and that's her one salvation now—that she isn't self-conscious. You see, it's only the fault of her environment and training, after all. It isn't her heart that's wrong."

"Indeed it isn't!"

"It will be different when she is older—when she has seen a little more of the world outside Hampden Falls. She'll go to school, of course, and I think she ought to travel a little. Meanwhile, she mustn't live—just like this, though; certainly not for a time, at least."

"No, no, I'm afraid not," agreed William, perplexedly, rising to his feet. "But we must think—what can be done." His step was even slower than usual as he left the room, and his eyes were troubled.

CHAPTER XV

WHAT BERTRAM CALLS "THE LIMIT"

At half past ten o'clock on the evening following Mrs. Stetson's very plain talk with William, the telephone bell at the Beacon Street house rang sharply. Pete answered it.

"Well?"—Pete never said "hello."

"Hello. Is that you, Pete?" called Billy's voice agitatedly. "Is Uncle William there?"

"No, Miss Billy."

"Oh dear! Well, Mr. Cyril, then?"

"He's out, too, Miss Billy. And Mr. Bertram—they're all out."

"Yes, yes, I know HE'S out," almost sobbed Billy. "Dear, dear, what shall I do! Pete, you'll have to come. There isn't any other way!"

"Yes, Miss; where?" Pete's voice was dubious, but respectful.

"To the Boylston Street subway—on the Common, you

know—North-bound side. I'll wait for you—but HURRY! You see, I'm all alone here."

"Alone! Miss Billy—in the subway at this time of night! But, Miss Billy, you shouldn't—you can't—you mustn't—" stuttered the old man in helpless horror.

"Yes, yes, Pete, but never mind; I am here! And I should think if 'twas such a dreadful thing you would hurry FAST to get here, so I wouldn't be alone," appealed Billy.

With an inarticulate cry Pete jerked the receiver on to the hook, and stumbled away from the telephone. Five minutes later he had left the house and was hurrying through the Common to the Boylston Street subway station.

Billy, a long cloak thrown over her white dress, was waiting for him. Her white slippers tapped the platform nervously, and her hair, under the light scarf of lace, fluffed into little broken curls as if it had been blown by the wind.

"Miss Billy, Miss Billy, what can this mean?" gasped the man. "Where is Mrs. Stetson?"

"At Mrs. Hartwell's—you know she is giving a reception tonight. But come, we must hurry! I'm after Mr. Bertram."

"After Mr. Bertram!"

"Yes, yes."

"Alone?—like this?"

"But I'm not alone now; I have you. Don't you see?"

At the blank stupefaction in the man's face, the girl

sighed impatiently.

"Dear me! I suppose I'll have to explain; but we're losing time—and we mustn't—we mustn't!" she cried feverishly. "Listen then, quick. It was at Mrs. Hartwell's tonight. I'd been watching Mr. Bertram. He was with that horrid Mr. Seaver, and I never liked him, never! I overheard something they said, about some place they were going to, and I didn't like what Mr. Seaver said. I tried to speak to Mr. Bertram, but I didn't get a chance; and the next thing I knew he'd gone with that Seaver man! I saw them just in time to snatch my cloak and follow them."

"FOLLOW them! MISS BILLY!"

"I had to, Pete; don't you see? There was no one else. Mr. Cyril and Uncle William had gone—home, I supposed. I sent back word by the maid to Aunt Hannah that I'd gone ahead; you know the carriage was ordered for eleven; but I'm afraid she won't have sense to tell Aunt Hannah, she looked so dazed and frightened when I told her. But I COULDN'T wait to say more. Well, I hurried out and caught up with Mr. Bertram just as they were crossing Arlington Street to the Garden. I'd heard them say they were going to walk, so I knew I could do it. But, Pete, after I got there, I didn't dare to speak—I didn't DARE to! So I just—followed. They went straight through the Garden and across the Common to Tremont Street, and on and on until they stopped and went down some stairs, all marble and lights and mirrors. 'Twas a restaurant, I think. I saw just where it was, then I flew back here to telephone for Uncle William. I knew HE could do something. But—well, you know the rest. I had to take you. Now come, quick; I'll show you."

"But, Miss Billy, I can't! You mustn't; it's impossible," chattered old Pete. "Come, let me take ye home, Miss Billy, do!"

"Home—and leave Mr. Bertram with that Seaver man? No, no!"

"What CAN ye do?"

"Do? I can get him to come home with me, of course."

The old man made a despairing gesture and looked about him as if for help. He saw then the curious, questioning eyes on all sides; and with a quick change of manner, he touched Miss Billy's arm.

"Yes; we'll go. Come," he apparently agreed. But once outside on the broad expanse before the Subway entrance he stopped again. "Miss Billy, please come home," he implored. "Ye don't know—ye can't know what yer a-doin'!"

The girl tossed her head. She was angry now.

"Pete, if you will not go with me I shall go alone. I am not afraid."

"But the hour—the place—you, a young girl! Miss Billy!" remonstrated the old man agitatedly.

"It isn't so very late. I've been out lots of times later than this at home. And as for the place, it's all light and bright, and lots of people were going in—ladies and gentlemen. Nothing could hurt me, Pete, and I shall go; but I'd rather you were with me. Why, Pete, we mustn't leave him. He isn't—he isn't HIMSELF, Pete. He—he's been DRINKING!" Billy's voice broke, and her face flushed scarlet. She was almost crying. "Come, you won't refuse now!" she finished, resolutely turning toward the street.

And because old Pete could not pick her up bodily and carry her home, he followed close at her heels. At the head of the marble stairs "all lights and mirrors," however, he made one last plea.

"Miss Billy, once more I beg of ye, won't ye come home? Ye don't know what yer a-doin', Miss Billy, ye don't—ye don't!"

"I can't go home," persisted Billy. "I must get Mr. Bertram away from that man. Now come; we'll just stand at the door and look in until we see him. Then I'll go straight to him and speak to him." And with that she turned and ran down the steps.

Billy blinked a little at the lights which, reflected in the great plate-glass mirrors, were a million dazzling points that found themselves again repeated in the sparkling crystal and glittering silver on the flower-decked tables. All about her Billy saw flushed-faced men, and bright-eyed women, laughing, chatting, and clinking together their slender-stemmed wine glasses. But nowhere, as she looked about her, could Billy descry the man she sought.

The head waiter came forward with uplifted hand, but Billy did not see him. A girl at her left laughed disagreeably, and several men stared with boldly admiring eyes; but to them, too, Billy paid no heed. Then, halfway across the room she spied Bertram and Seaver sitting together at a small table alone.

Simultaneously her own and Bertram's eyes met.

With a sharp word under his breath Bertram sprang to his feet. His befogged brain had cleared suddenly under the shock of Billy's presence.

"Billy, for Heaven's sake what are you doing here?" he

Eleanor H. Porter

demanded in a low voice, as he reached her side.

"I came for you. I want you to go home with me, please, Mr. Bertram," whispered Billy, pleadingly.

The man had not waited for an answer to his question. With a deft touch he had turned Billy toward the door; and even as she finished her sentence she found herself in the marble hallway confronting Pete, pallid-faced, and shaking.

"And you, too, Pete! Great Scott! what does this mean?" he exploded angrily.

Pete could only shake his head and glance imploringly at Billy. His dry lips and tongue refused to articulate even one word.

"We came—for—you," choked Billy. "You see, I don't like that Seaver man."

"Well, by Jove! this is the limit!" breathed Bertram.

CHAPTER XVI

KATE TAKES A HAND

Undeniably Billy was in disgrace, and none knew it better than Billy herself. The whole family had contributed to this knowledge. Aunt Hannah was inexpressibly shocked; she had not breath even to ejaculate "My grief and conscience!" Kate was disgusted; Cyril was coldly reserved; Bertram was frankly angry; even William was vexed, and showed it. Spunk, too, as if in league with the rest, took this opportunity to display one of his occasional fits of independence; and when Billy, longing for some sort of comfort, called him to her, he settled back on his tiny haunches and imperturbably winked and blinked his indifference.

Nearly all the family had had something to say to Billy on the matter, with not entirely satisfactory results, when Kate determined to see what she could do. She chose a time when she could have the girl quite to herself with small likelihood of interruption.

"But, Billy, how could you do such an absurd thing?" she demanded. "The idea of leaving my house alone, at half-past ten at night, to follow a couple of men through the streets of Boston, and then with my brothers' butler make a scene like that in a—a public dining-room!"

Billy sighed in a discouraged way.

"Aunt Kate, can't I make you and the rest of them understand that I didn't start out to do all that? I meant just to speak to Mr. Bertram, and get him away from that man."

"But, my dear child, even that was bad enough!"

Billy lifted her chin.

"You don't seem to think, Aunt Kate; Mr. Bertram was—was not sober."

"All the more reason then why you should NOT have done what you did!"

"Why, Aunt Kate, you wouldn't leave him alone in that condition with that man!"

It was Mrs. Hartwell's turn to sigh.

"But, Billy," she contested, wearily, "can't you understand that it wasn't YOUR place to interfere—you, a young girl?"

"I'm sure I don't see what difference that makes. I was the only one that could do it! Besides, afterward, I did try to get some one else, Uncle William and Mr. Cyril. But when I found I couldn't get them, I just had to do it alone—that is, with Pete."

"Pete!" scoffed Mrs. Hartwell. "Pete, indeed!"

Billy's head came up with a jerk. Billy was very angry now.

"Aunt Kate, it seems I've done a very terrible thing, but I'm sure I don't see it that way. I wasn't afraid, and I wasn't in the least bit of danger anywhere. I knew my way perfectly, and I did NOT make any 'scene' in that restaurant. I just asked Mr. Bertram to come home with me. One would think you WANTED Mr. Bertram to go off with that man and—and drink too much. But Uncle William hasn't liked him before, not one bit! I've heard him talk about him—that Mr. Seaver."

Mrs. Hartwell raised both her hands, palms outward.

"Billy, it is useless to talk with you. You are quite impossible. It is even worse than I expected!" she cried, with wrathful impatience.

"Worse than you—expected? What do you mean, please?"

"Worse than I thought it would be—before you came. The idea of those five men taking a girl to bring up!"

Billy sat very still. She was even holding her breath, though Mrs. Hartwell did not know that.

"You mean—that they did not—want me?" she asked quietly, so quietly that Mrs. Hartwell did not realize the sudden tension behind the words. For that matter, Mrs. Hartwell was too angry now to realize anything outside of herself.

"Want you! Billy, it is high time that you understand just how things are, and have been, at the house; then perhaps you will conduct yourself with an eye a little more to other people's comfort. Can you imagine three young men like my brothers WANTING to take a strange young woman into their home to upset everything?"

"To—upset—everything!" echoed Billy, faintly. "And have I done—that?"

"Of course you have! How could you help it? To begin with, they thought you were a boy, and that was bad enough; but William was so anxious to do right by his dead friend that he insisted upon taking you, much against the will of all the rest of us. Oh, I know this isn't pleasant for you to hear," admitted Mrs. Hartwell, in response to the dismayed expression in Billy's eyes; "but I think it's high time you realize something of what those men have sacrificed for you. Now, to resume. When they found you were a girl, what did they do? Did they turn you over to some school or such place, as they should have done? Certainly not! William would not hear of it. He turned Bertram out of his rooms, put you into them, and established Aunt Hannah as chaperon and me as substitute until she arrived. But because, through it all, he smiled blandly, you have been blind to the whole thing.

"And what is the result? His entire household routine is shattered to atoms. You have accepted the whole house as if it were your own. You take Cyril's time to teach you music, and Bertram's to teach you painting, without a thought of what it means to them. There! I suppose I ought not to have said all this, but I couldn't help it, Billy. And surely now, NOW you appreciate a little more what your coming to this house has meant, and what my brothers have done for you."

"I do, certainly," said Billy, still in that voice that was so oddly smooth and emotionless.

"And you'll try to be more tractable, less headstrong, less assertive of your presence?"

The girl sprang to her feet now.

"More tractable! Less assertive of my presence!" she cried. "Mrs. Hartwell, do you mean to say you think I'd STAY after what you've told me?"

"Stay? Why, of course you'll stay! Don't be silly, child. I didn't tell you this to make you go. I only wanted you to understand how things were—and are."

"And I do understand—and I'm going."

Mrs. Hartwell frowned. Her face changed color.

"Come, come, Billy, this is nonsense. William wants you here. He would never forgive me if anything I said should send you away. You must not be angry with, him."

Billy turned now like an enraged little tigress.

"Angry with him! Why, I love him—I love them all! They are the dearest men ever, and they've been so good to me!" The girl's voice broke a little, then went on with a more determined ring. "Do you think I'd have them know why I'm going?—that I'd hurt them like that? Never!"

"But, Billy, what are you going to do?"

"I don't know. I've got to plan it out. I only know now that I'm going, sure!" And with a choking little cry Billy ran from the room.

In her own chamber a minute later the tears fell unrestrained.

"It's home—all the home there is—anywhere!" she sobbed. "But it's got to go—it's got to go!"

CHAPTER XVII

A PINK-RIBBON TRAIL

Mrs. Stetson wore an air of unmistakable relief as she stepped into William's sitting-room. Even her knock at the half-open door had sounded almost triumphant.

"William, it does seem as if Fate itself had intervened to help us out," she began delightedly. "Billy, of her own accord, came to me this morning, and said that she wanted to go away with me for a little trip. So you see that will make it easier for us."

"Good! That is fortunate, indeed," cried William; but his voice did not carry quite the joy that his words expressed. "I have been disturbed ever since your remarks the other day," he continued wearily; "and of course her extraordinary escapade the next evening did not help matters any. It is better, I know, that she shouldn't be here—for a time. Though I shall miss her terribly. But, tell me, what is it—what does she want to do?"

"She says she guesses she is homesick for Hampden Falls; that she'd like to go back there for a few weeks this summer if I'll go with her. The—the dear child seems suddenly to have taken a great fancy to me," explained Aunt Hannah, unsteadily. "I never saw her so affectionate."

"She is a dear girl—a very dear girl; and she has a warm heart." William cleared his throat sonorously, but even that did not clear his voice. "It was her heart that led her wrong the other night," he declared. "Hers was a brave and fearless act—but a very unwise one. Much as I deplore Bertram's intimacy with Seaver, I should hesitate to take the course marked out by Billy. Bertram is not a child. But tell me more of this trip of yours. How did Billy happen to suggest it?"

"I don't know. I noticed yesterday that she seemed strangely silent—unhappy, in fact. She sat alone in her room the greater part of the day, and I could not get her out of it. But this morning she came to my door as bright as the sun itself and made me the proposition I told you of. She says her aunt's house is closed, awaiting its sale; but that she would like to open it for awhile this summer, if I'd like to go. Naturally, you can understand that I'd very quickly fall in with a plan like that—one which promised so easily to settle our difficulties."

"Yes, of course, of course," muttered William. "It is very fine, very fine indeed," he concluded. And again his voice failed quite to match his words in enthusiasm.

"Then I'll go and begin to see to my things," murmured Mrs. Stetson, rising to her feet. "Billy seems anxious to get away."

Billy did, indeed, seem anxious to get away. She announced her intended departure at once to the family. She called it a visit to her old home, and she seemed very glad in her preparations. If there was anything forced in this gayety, no one noticed it, or at least, no one spoke of it. The family saw very little of Billy, indeed, these days. She said that she was busy; that she had packing to do. She stopped taking lessons of Cyril, and visited Bertram's studio only once during the whole three days before she went away, and then merely to get some things that belonged to her. On the fourth day, almost before the family realized what was happening, she was gone; and with her had gone Mrs. Stetson and Spunk.

The family said they liked it—the quiet, the freedom. They said they liked to be alone—all but William. He said nothing.

And yet—

When Bertram went to his studio that morning he did not pick up his brushes until he had sat for long minutes before the sketch of a red-cheeked, curly-headed young girl whose eyes held a peculiarly wistful appeal; and Cyril, at his piano up-stairs, sat with idle fingers until they finally drifted into a simple little melody—the last thing Billy had been learning.

It was Pete who brought in the kitten; and Billy had been gone a whole week then.

"The poor little beast was cryin' at the alleyway door, sir," he explained. "I—I made so bold as to bring him in."

"Of course," said William. "Did you feed it?"

"Yes, sir; Ling did."

There was a pause, then Pete spoke, diffidently.

"I thought, sir, if ye didn't mind, I'd keep it. I'll try to see that it stays down-stairs, sir, out of yer way."

"That's all right, Pete; keep it, by all means, by all means," approved William.

"Thank ye, sir. Ye see, it's a stray. It hasn't got any home. And, did ye notice, sir? it looks like Spunk."

"Yes, I noticed," said William, stirring with sudden restlessness. "I noticed."

"Yes, sir," said Pete. And he turned and carried the small gray cat away.

The new kitten did not stay down-stairs. Pete tried, it is true, to keep his promise to watch it; but after he had seen the little animal carried surreptitiously up-stairs in Mr. William's arms, he relaxed his vigilance. Some days later the kitten appeared with a huge pink bow behind its ears, somewhat awkwardly tied, if it must be confessed. Where it came from, or who put it there was not known—until one day the kitten was found in the hall delightedly chewing at the end of what had been a roll of pink ribbon. Up the stairs led a trail of pink ribbon and curling white paper—and the end of the trail was in William's room.

CHAPTER XVIII

BILLY WRITES ANOTHER LETTER

By the middle of June only William and the gray kitten were left with Pete and Dong Ling in the Beacon Street house. Cyril had sailed for England, and Bertram had gone on a sketching trip with a friend.

To William the house this summer was unusually lonely; indeed, he found the silent, deserted rooms almost unbearable. Even the presence of the little gray cat served only to accentuate the loneliness—it reminded him of Billy.

William missed Billy. He owned that now even to Pete. He said that he would be glad when she came back. To himself he said that he wished he had not fallen in quite so readily with Aunt Hannah's notion of getting the child away. It was all nonsense, he declared. All she needed was a little curbing and directing, both of which could just as well have been done there at home. But she had gone, and it could not be helped now. The only thing left for him to do was to see that it did not occur again. When Billy came back she should stay, except for necessary absences for school, of course. All this William settled in his own mind quite to his own satisfaction, entirely forgetting, strange to say, that it had been Billy's own suggestion that she go away.

Very promptly William wrote to Billy. He told her how he missed her, and said that he had stopped trying to sort and catalogue his collections until she should be there to help him. He told her, too, after a time, of the gray kitten, "Spunkie," that looked so much like Spunk.

In reply he received plump white envelopes directed in the round, schoolboy hand that he remembered so well. In the envelopes were letters, cheery and entertaining, like Billy herself. They thanked him for all his many kindnesses, and they told him something of what Billy was doing. They showed unbounded interest in the new kitten, and in all else that William wrote about; but they hinted very plainly that he had better not wait for her to help him out on the catalogue, for it would soon be autumn, and she would be in school.

William frowned at this, and shook his head; yet he knew that it was true.

In August William closed the Beacon street house and went to the Rangeley Lakes on a camping trip. He told himself that he would not go had it not been for a promise given to an old college friend months before. True, he had been anticipating this trip all winter; but it occurred to him now that it would be much more interesting to go to Hampden Falls and see Billy. He had been to the Rangeley Lakes, and he had not been to Hampden Falls; besides, there would be Ned Harding and those queer old maids with their shaded house and socketed chairs to see. In short, to William, at the moment, there seemed no place quite so absorbingly interesting as was Hampden Falls. But he went to the Rangeley Lakes.

In September Cyril came back from Europe, and Bertram from the Adirondacks where he had been spending the month of August. William already had arrived, and with Pete and Dong Ling had opened the house.

"Where's Billy? Isn't Billy here?" demanded Bertram.

"No. She isn't back yet," replied William.

"You don't mean to say she's stayed up there all summer!" exclaimed Cyril.

"Why, yes, I—I suppose so," hesitated William. "You see, I haven't heard but once for a month. I've been down in Maine, you know."

William wrote to Billy that night.

"My dear:—" he said in part. "I hope you'll come home right away. We want to see SOMETHING of you before you go away again, and you know the schools will be opening soon.

"By the way, it has just occurred to me as I write that perhaps, after all, you won't have to go quite away. There are plenty of good schools for young ladies right in and near Boston, which I am sure you could attend, and still live at home. Suppose you come back then as soon as you can, and we'll talk it up. And that reminds me, I wonder how Spunk will get along with Spunkie. Spunkie has been boarding out all August at a cat home, but he seems glad to get back to us. I am anxious to see the two little chaps together, just to find out how much alike they really do look."

Very promptly came Billy's answer; but William's face, after he had read the letter, was almost as blank as it had been on that April day when Billy's first letter came—though this time for a far different reason.

"Why, boys, she—isn't—coming," he announced in dismay.

"Isn't coming!" ejaculated two astonished Voices.

"No."

"Not—at—ALL?"

"Why, of course, later," retorted William, with unwonted sharpness. "But not now. This is what she says." And he read aloud:

"DEAR UNCLE WILLIAM:—You poor dear man! Did you think I'd really let you spend your time and your thought over hunting up a school for me, after all the rest you have done for me? Not a bit of it! Why, Aunt Hannah and I have been buried under school catalogues all summer, and I have studied them all until I know just which has turkey dinners on Sundays, and which ice cream at least twice a week. And it's all settled, too, long ago. I'm going to a girls' school up the Hudson a little way—a lovely place, I'm sure, from the pictures of it.

"Oh, and another thing; I shall go right from here. Two girls at Hampden Falls are going, and I shall go with them. Isn't that a fine chance for me? You see it would never do, anyway, for me to go alone—me, a 'Billy'— unless I sent a special courier ahead to announce that 'Billy' was a girl.

"Aunt Hannah has decided to stay here this winter in the old house. She likes it ever so much, and I don't think I shall sell the place just yet, anyway. She will go back, of course, to Boston (after I've gone) to get some things at the house that she'll want, and also to do some shopping. But she'll let you know when she'll be there.

"I'll write more later, but just now I'm in a terrible rush. I only write this note to set your poor heart at rest about having to hunt up a school for me.

"With love to all,

"BILLY."

As had happened once before after a letter from Billy had been read, there was a long pause.

"Well, by Jove!" breathed Bertram.

"It's very sensible, I'm sure," declared Cyril. "Still, I must confess, I would have liked to pick out her piano teacher for her."

William said nothing—perhaps because he was reading Billy's letter again.

At eight o'clock that night Bertram tapped on Cyril's door.

"What's the trouble?" demanded Cyril in answer to the look on the other's face.

Bertram lifted his eyebrows oddly.

"I'm not sure whether you'll call it 'trouble' or not," he replied; "but I think it's safe to say that Billy is gone—for good."

"For good! What do you mean?—that she's not coming back —ever?"

"Exactly that."

"Nonsense! What's put that notion into your head?"

"Billy's letter first; after that, Pete."

"Pete!"

"Yes. He came to me a few minutes ago, looking as if he had seen a ghost. It seems he swept Billy's rooms this morning and put them in order against her coming; and tonight William told him that she wouldn't be here at present. Pete came straight to me. He said he didn't dare tell Mr. William, but he'd got to tell some one: there wasn't one single thing of Miss Billy's left in her rooms nor anywhere else in the house—not so much as a handkerchief or a hairpin."

"Hm-m; that does look—suspicious," murmured Cyril. "What's up, do you think?"

"Don't know; but something, sure. Still, of course we may be wrong. We won't say anything to Will about it, anyhow. Poor old chap, 'twould worry him, specially if he thought Billy's feelings had been hurt."

"Hurt?—nonsense! Why, we did everything for her— everything!"

"Yes, I know—and she tried to do EVERYTHING for us, too," retorted Bertram, quizzically, as he turned away.

CHAPTER XIX

SEEING BILLY OFF

Early in October Mrs. Stetson arrived at the Beacon Street house, but she did not stay long.

"I've come for just a few things I want, and to do some shopping," she explained.

"But Aunt Hannah," remonstrated William, "what is the meaning of this? Why are you staying up there at Hampden Falls?"

"I like it there, William; and why shouldn't I stay? Surely there's no need for me to be here now, with Billy away!"

"But Billy's coming back!"

"Of course she's coming back," laughed Aunt Hannah, "but not this winter, certainly. Why, William, what's the matter? I'm sure, I think it's a beautiful arrangement. Why, don't you remember? It's just what we said we wanted—to keep Billy away for awhile. And the best part of it is, it's her own idea from the start."

"Yes, I know, I know," frowned William: "but I'm not sure,

after all, that that idea of ours wasn't a mistake,—a mistake that she needed to get away."

"Never! We were just right about it," declared Aunt Hannah, with conviction.

"And is Billy—happy?"

"She seems to be."

"Hm-m; well, THAT'S good," said William, as he turned to go up to his room. But as he climbed the stairs he sighed; and to hear him, one would have thought it anything but good to him—that Billy was happy.

One by one the weeks passed. Mrs. Stetson had long since gone back to Hampden Falls; and Bertram said that the Strata was beginning to look natural again. There remained now, indeed, only Spunkie, the small gray cat, to remind any one of the days that were gone—though, to be sure, there were Billy's letters, if they might be called a reminder.

Billy did not write often. She said that she was "too busy to breathe." Such letters as did come from her were addressed to William, though they soon came to be claimed by the entire family. Bertram and Cyril frankly demanded that William read them aloud; and even Pete always contrived to have some dusting or "puttering" within earshot—a subterfuge quite well understood, but never reproved by any of the brothers.

When the Christmas vacation drew near, William wrote that he hoped Billy and Aunt Hannah would spend it with them; but Billy answered that although she appreciated their kindness and thanked them for it, yet she must decline their invitation, as she had already invited several of the girls to go home with her to Hampden Falls for a country Christmas.

For the Easter vacation William was even more insistent—but so was Billy: she had already accepted an invitation to go home with one of the girls, and she did not think it would be at all polite to change her plans now.

William fretted not a little. Even Cyril and Bertram said that it was "too bad"; that they themselves would like to see the girl—so they would!

It was in the spring, at the close of school, however, that the heaviest blow fell: Billy was not coming to Boston even then. She wrote that she and Aunt Hannah were going to "run across the water for a little trip through the British Isles"; and that their passage was already engaged.

"And so you see," she explained, "I shall not have a minute to spare. There'll be only time to skip home for Aunt Hannah, and to pack the trunks before it'll be time to start."

Bertram looked at Cyril significantly when this letter was read aloud; and afterward he muttered in Cyril's ear:

"You see! It's Hampden Falls she calls 'home' now—not the Strata."

"Yes, I see," frowned Cyril. "It does look suspicious."

Two days before the date of Billy's expected sailing, William announced at the breakfast table that he was going away on business; might be gone until the end of the week.

"You don't say," commented Bertram. "I'M going to-morrow, but I'm coming back in a couple of days."

"Hm-m;" murmured William, abstractedly. "Oh, well, I may be back before the end of the week."

Only one meal did Cyril eat alone after his brothers had gone; then he told Pete that he had decided to take the night boat for New York. There was a little matter that called him there, he said, and he believed the trip by water would be a pleasure, the night was so fine and warm.

In New York Cyril had little trouble in finding Billy, as he knew the steamship she was to take.

"I thought as long as I was in New York to-day I'd just come and say good-by to you and Aunt Hannah," he informed her, with an evident aim toward making his presence appear to be casual.

"That was good of you!" exclaimed Billy. "And how are Uncle William and Mr. Bertram?"

"Very well, I fancy, though they weren't there when I left," replied the man.

"Oh!—gone away?"

"Yes. A little matter of business they said; but—well, by Jove!" he broke off, his gaze on a familiar figure hurrying at that moment toward them. "There's William now!"

William, with no eyes but for Billy, came rapidly forward.

"Well, well, Billy! I thought as long as I happened to be in New York to-day I'd just run down to the boat and see you and Aunt Hannah off, and wish—CYRIL! Where did YOU come from?"

Eleanor H. Porter

Billy laughed.

"He just happened to be in town, too, Uncle William, like you," she explained. "And I'm sure I think it's lovely of you to be so kind. Aunt Hannah'll be up right away. She went down to the stateroom to—" This time it was Billy who stopped abruptly. The two men facing her could not see what she saw, and not until their brother Bertram's merry greeting fell on their ears did they understand her sudden silence.

"And is this the way you meant to run away from us, young lady?" cried Bertram. "Not so fast! You see, I happened to be in New York this morning, and so I—" Something in Billy's face sent a pause to his words just as his eyes spied the two men at the girl's side. For a moment he stared dumbly; then he gave a merry gesture of defeat.

"It's all up! I might as well confess. I'VE been planning this thing for three weeks, Billy, ever since your letter came, in fact. As for my two fellow-sinners here, I'll wager they weren't two days behind me in their planning. So now, own up, boys!"

William and Cyril, however, did not have to "own up." Mrs. Stetson appeared at the moment and created, for them, a very welcome diversion.

Long minutes later, when the good-byes had become nothing but a flutter of white handkerchiefs from deck to shore, and shore to deck, William drew a long sigh.

"That's a nice little girl, boys, a nice little girl!" he exclaimed. "I declare! I didn't suppose I'd mind so much her going so far away."

CHAPTER XX

BILLY, THE MYTH

To all appearances it came about very naturally that Billy did not return to America for some time. During the summer she wrote occasionally to William, and gave glowing accounts of their travels. Then in September came the letter telling him that they had concluded to stay through the winter in Paris. Billy wrote that she had decided not to go to college. She would take up some studies there in Paris, she said, but she would devote herself more particularly to her music.

When the next summer came there was still something other than America to claim her attention: the Calderwells had invited her to cruise with them for three months. Their yacht was a little floating palace of delight, Billy declared, not to mention the charm of the unknown lands and waters that she and Aunt Hannah would see.

Of all this Billy wrote to William—at occasional intervals—but she did not come home. Even when the next autumn came, there was still Paris to detain her for another long winter of study.

In the Henshaw house on Beacon Street, William mourned not a little as each recurring season brought no Billy.

Eleanor H. Porter

"The idea! It's just as if one didn't have a namesake!" he fumed.

"Well, did you have one?" Bertram demanded one day. "Really, Will, I'm beginning to think she's a myth. Long years ago, from the first of April till June we did have two frolicsome sprites here that announced themselves as 'Billy' and 'Spunk,' I'll own. And a year later, by ways devious and secret, we three managed to see the one called 'Billy' off on a great steamship. Since then, what? A word—a message—a scrap of paper. Billy's a myth, I say!"

William sighed.

"Sometimes I don't know but you are right," he admitted. "Why, it'll be three years next June since Billy was here. She must be nearly twenty-one—and we know almost nothing about her."

"That's so. I wonder—" Bertram paused, and laughed a little, "I wonder if NOW she'd play guardian angel to me through the streets of Boston."

William threw a keen glance into his brother's face.

"I don't believe it would be quite necessary, NOW, Bert," he said quietly.

The other flushed a little, but his eyes softened.

"Maybe not, Will; still—one can always find some use for— a guardian angel, you know," he finished, almost under his breath.

To Cyril Bertram had occasionally spoken, during the last two years, of their first suspicions concerning Billy's absence. They speculated vaguely, too, as to why she had gone, and if she would ever come back; and they wondered if anything could have wounded her and sent her away. To William they said nothing of all this, however; though they agreed that they would have asked Kate for her opinion, had she been there. But Kate was not there. As it chanced, a good business opportunity had called Kate's husband to a Western town very soon after Billy herself had gone to Hampden Falls; and since the family's removal to the West, Mrs. Hartwell had not once returned to Boston.

It was in April, three years since Billy's first appearance in the Beacon Street house, that Bertram met his friend, Hugh Calderwell, on the street one afternoon, and brought him home to dinner.

Hugh Calderwell was a youth who, Bertram said, had been born with a whole dozen silver spoons in his mouth. And, indeed, it would seem so, if present prosperity were any indication. He was a good-looking young fellow with a frank manliness that appealed to men, and a deferential chivalry that appealed to women; a combination that brought him many friends—and some enemies. With plenty of money to indulge a passion for traveling, young Calderwell had spent the most of his time since graduation in daring trips into the heart of almost impenetrable forests, or to the top of almost inaccessible mountains, with an occasional more ordinary trip to give variety. He had now come to the point, however, where he was determined to "settle down to something that meant something," he told the Henshaws, as the four men smoked in Bertram's den after dinner.

"Yes, sir, I have," he iterated. "And, by the way, the little girl that has set me to thinking in such good earnest is a friend of yours, too,—Miss Neilson. I met her in Paris. She was on our yacht all last summer."

Three men sat suddenly erect in their chairs.

"Billy?" cried three voices. "Do you know Billy?"

"To be sure! And you do, too, she says."

"Oh, no, we don't," disputed Bertram, emphatically. "But we WISH we did!"

His guest laughed.

"Well, I fancy you DO know her, or you wouldn't have answered like that," he retorted. "For you just begin to know Miss Billy when you find out that you DON'T know her. She is a charming girl—a very charming girl."

"She is my namesake," announced William, in what Bertram called his "finest ever" voice that he used only for the choicest bits in his collections.

"Yes, she told me," smiled Calderwell. "'Billy' for 'William.' Odd idea, too, but clever. It helps to distinguish her even more—though she doesn't need it, for that matter."

"'Doesn't need it,'" echoed William in a puzzled voice.

"No. Perhaps you don't know, Mr. Henshaw, but Miss Billy is a very popular young woman. You have reason to be proud of your namesake."

"I have always been that," declared William, with just a touch of hauteur.

"Tell us about her," begged Bertram. "You remember I said that we wished we did know her."

Calderwell smiled.

"I don't believe, after all, that you do know much about her," he began musingly. "Billy is not one who talks much of herself, I fancy, in her letters."

William frowned. This time there was more than a touch of hauteur in his voice.

"MISS NEILSON is not one to show vanity anywhere," he said, with suggestive emphasis on the name.

"Indeed she isn't," agreed Calderwell, heartily. "She is a fine girl—quite one of the finest I know, in fact."

There was an uncomfortable silence. Over in the corner Cyril puffed at his cigar with an air almost of boredom. He had not spoken since his first surprised questioning with the others, "Do you know Billy?" William was still frowning. Even Bertram wore a look that was not quite satisfied.

"Miss Neilson has spent two winters in Paris now, you know," resumed Calderwell, after a moment; "and she is very popular both with the American colony, and with the other students. As for her 'Aunt Hannah'—they all make a pet of her; but that is, perhaps, because Billy herself is so devoted."

Again William frowned at the familiar "Billy"; but Calderwell talked on unheeding.

"After all, I'm not sure but some of us regard 'Aunt Hannah' with scant favor, occasionally," he laughed; "something as if she were the dragon that guarded the princess, you know. Miss Billy IS popular with the men, and she has suitors enough to turn any girl's head—but her own."

"Suitors!" cried William, plainly aghast. "Why, Billy's nothing but a child!"

Calderwell gave an odd smile.

"How long is it since you've seen—Miss Neilson?" he asked.

"Two years."

"And then only for a few minutes just before she sailed," amended Bertram. "We haven't really seen much of her since three years ago."

"Hm-m; well, you'll see for yourself soon. You know she's coming home next month."

Not one of the brothers did know it—but not one of them intended that Calderwell should find out that they did not.

"Yes, she's coming home," said William, lifting his chin a little.

"Oh, yes, next month," added Bertram, nonchalantly.

Even Cyril across the room was not to be outdone.

"Yes. Miss Neilson comes home next month," he said.

CHAPTER XXI

BILLY, THE REALITY

Very early in May came the cheery letter from Billy herself announcing the news of her intended return.

"And I shall be so glad to see you all," she wrote in closing. "It seems so long since I left America." Then she signed her name with "kindest regards to all"—Billy did not send "love to all" any more.

William at once began to make plans for his namesake's comfort.

"But, Will, she didn't say she was coming here," Bertram reminded him.

"She didn't need to," smiled William, confidently. "She just took it for granted, of course. This is her home."

"But it hasn't been—for years. She's called Hampden Falls 'home.'"

"I know, but that was before," demurred William, his eyes a little anxious. "Besides, they've sold the house now, you know. There's nowhere for her to go but here, Bertram."

Eleanor H. Porter

"All right," acquiesced the younger man, still doubtingly. "Maybe that's so; maybe! But—" he did not finish his sentence, and his eyes were troubled as he watched his brother begin to rearrange Billy's rooms. In time, however, so sure was William of Billy's return to the Beacon Street house, that Bertram ceased to question; and, with almost as much confidence as William himself displayed, he devoted his energies to the preparations for Billy's arrival.

And what preparations they were! Even Cyril helped this time to the extent of placing on Billy's piano a copy of his latest book, and a pile of new music. Nor were the melodies that floated down from the upper floor akin to funeral marches; they were perilously near to being allied to "ragtime."

At last everything was ready. There was not one more bit of dust to catch Pete's eye, nor one more adornment that demanded William's careful hand to adjust. In Billy's rooms new curtains graced the windows and new rugs the floors. In Mrs. Stetson's, too, similar changes had been made. The latest and best "Face of a Girl" smiled at one from above Billy's piano, and the very rarest of William's treasures adorned the mantelpiece. No guns nor knives nor fishing-rods met the eyes now. Instead, at every turn, there was a hint of feminine tastes: a mirror, a workbasket, a low sewing-chair, a stand with a tea tray. And everywhere were roses, up-stairs and down-stairs, until the air was heavy with their perfume. In the dining-room Pete was again "swinging back and forth like a pendulum," it is true; but it was a cheerful pendulum to-day, anxious only that no time should be lost. In the kitchen alone was there unhappiness, and there because Dong Ling had already spoiled a whole cake of chocolate in a vain attempt to make Billy's favorite fudge. Even Spunkie, grown now to be sleek, lazy, and majestically indifferent, was in holiday attire, for a brand-new pink bow of huge dimensions adorned his fat neck—for the first time in many months.

"You see," William had explained to Bertram, "I put on that ribbon again because I thought it would make Spunkie seem more homelike, and more like Spunk. You know there wasn't anything Billy missed so much as that kitten when she went abroad. Aunt Hannah said so."

"Yes, I know," Bertram had laughed; "but still, Spunkie isn't Spunk, you understand!" he had finished, with a vision in his eyes of Billy as she had looked that first night when she had triumphantly lifted from the green basket the little gray kitten with its enormous pink bow. This time there was no circuitous journeying, no secrecy in the trip to New York. Quite as a matter of course the three brother made their plans to meet Billy, and quite as a matter of course they met her. Perhaps the only cloud in the horizon of their happiness was the presence of Calderwell. He, too, had come to meet Billy—and all the Henshaw brothers were vaguely conscious of a growing feeling of dislike toward Calderwell.

Billy was unmistakably glad to see them—and to see Calderwell. It was while she was talking to Calderwell, indeed, that William and Cyril and Bertram had an opportunity really to see the girl, and to note what time had done for her. They knew then, at once, that time had been very kind.

It was a slim Billy that they saw, with a head royally poised, and a chin that was round and soft, and yet knew well its own mind. The eyes were still appealing, in a way, yet behind the appeal lay unsounded depths of—not one of the brothers could quite make up his mind just what, yet all the brothers determined to find out. The hair still curled distractingly behind the pretty ears, and fluffed into burnished bronze where the wind had loosened it. The cheeks were paler now, though the rose-flush still glowed warmly through the clear, smooth skin. The mouth—Billy's mouth had always been fascinating, Bertram suddenly decided, as he watched it now. He wanted to paint it—again. It was not too large for beauty nor too small for strength. It curved delightfully, and the lower lip had just the fullness and the color that he liked—to paint, he said to himself.

William, too, was watching Billy's mouth; in fact—though he did not know it—one never was long near Billy without noticing her mouth, if she talked. William thought it pretty, merry, and charmingly kissable; but just now he wished that it would talk to him, and not to Calderwell any longer. Cyril—indeed, Cyril was paying little attention to Billy. He had turned to Aunt Hannah. To tell the truth, it seemed to Cyril that, after all, Billy was very much like other merry, thoughtless, rather noisy young women, of whom he knew—and disliked—scores. It had occurred to him suddenly that perhaps it would not be unalloyed bliss to take this young namesake of William's home with them.

It was not until an hour later, when Billy, Aunt Hannah, and the Henshaws had reached the hotel where they were to spend the night, that the Henshaw brothers began really to get acquainted with Billy. She seemed then more like their own Billy—the Billy that they had known.

"And I'm so glad to be here," she cried; "and to see you all. America IS the best place, after all!"

"And of America, Boston is the Hub, you know," Bertram reminded her.

"It is," nodded Billy.

"And it hasn't changed a mite, except to grow better. You'll see to-morrow."

"As if I hadn't been counting the days!" she exulted. "And now what have you been doing—all of you?"

"Just wait till you see," laughed Bertram. "They're all spread out for your inspection."

"A new 'Face of a Girl'?"

"Of course—yards of them!"

"And heaps of 'Old Blues' and 'black basalts'?" she questioned, turning to William.

"Well, a—few," hesitated William, modestly.

"And—the music; what of that?" Billy looked now at Cyril.

"You'll see," he shrugged. "There's very little, after all—of anything."

Billy gave a wise shake of her head.

"I know better; and I want to see it all so much. We've talked and talked of it; haven't we, Aunt Hannah?—of what we would do when we got to Boston?"

"Yes, my dear; YOU have."

The girl laughed.

"I accept the amendment," she retorted with mock submission. "I suppose it is always I who talk."

"It was—when I painted you," teased Bertram. "By the way,

Eleanor H. Porter

I'll LET you talk if you'll pose again for me," he finished eagerly.

Billy uptilted her nose.

"Do you think, sir, you deserve it, after that speech?" she demanded.

"But how about YOUR art—your music?" entreated William. "You have said so little of that in your letters."

Billy hesitated. For a brief moment she glanced at Cyril. He did not appear to have heard his brother's question. He was talking with Aunt Hannah.

"Oh, I play—some," murmured the girl, almost evasively. "But tell me of yourself, Uncle William, and of what you are doing." And William needed no second bidding.

It was some time later that Billy turned to him with an amazed exclamation in response to something he had said.

"Home with you! Why, Uncle William, what do you mean? You didn't really think you'd got to be troubled with ME any longer!" she cried merrily.

William's face paled, then flushed.

"I did not call it 'trouble,' Billy," he said quietly. His grieved eyes looked straight into hers and drove the merriment quite away.

"Oh, I'm so sorry," she said gently. "And I appreciate your kindness, indeed I do; but I couldn't—really I couldn't think of such a thing!"

"And you don't have to think of it," cut in Bertram, who considered that the situation was becoming much too serious. "All you have to do is to come."

Billy shook her head.

"You are so good, all of you! But you didn't—you really didn't think I WAS—coming!" she protested.

"Indeed we did," asserted Bertram, promptly; "and we have done everything to get ready for you, too, even to rigging up Spunkie to masquerade as Spunk. I'll warrant that Pete's nose is already flattened against the window-pane, lest we should HAPPEN to come to-night; and there's no telling how many cakes of chocolate Dong Ling has spoiled by this time. We left him trying to make fudge, you know."

Billy laughed—but she cried, too; at least, her eyes grew suddenly moist. Bertram tried to decide afterward whether she laughed till she cried, or cried till she laughed.

"No, no," she demurred tremulously. "I couldn't. I really have never intended that."

"But why not? What are you going to do?" questioned William in a voice that was dazed and hurt.

The first question Billy ignored. The second she answered with a promptness and a gayety that was meant to turn the thoughts away from the first.

"We are going to Boston, Aunt Hannah and I. We've got rooms engaged for just now, but later we're going to take a house and live together. That's what we're going to do."

CHAPTER XXII

HUGH CALDERWELL

In the Beacon Street house William mournfully removed the huge pink bow from Spunkie's neck, and Bertram threw away the roses. Cyril marched up-stairs with his pile of new music and his book; and Pete, in obedience to orders, hid the workbasket, the tea table, and the low sewing-chair. With a great display of a "getting back home" air, Bertram moved many of his belongings upstairs—but inside of a week he had moved them down again, saying that, after all, he believed he liked the first floor better. Billy's rooms were closed then, and remained as they had for years—silent and deserted.

Billy with Aunt Hannah had gone directly to their Back Bay hotel. "This is for just while I'm house-hunting," the girl had said. But very soon she had decided to go to Hampden Falls for the summer and postpone her house-buying until the autumn. Billy was twenty-one now, and there were many matters of business to arrange with Lawyer Harding, concerning her inheritance. It was not until September, therefore, when Billy once more returned to Boston, that the Henshaw brothers had the opportunity of renewing their acquaintance with William's namesake.

"I want a home," Billy said to Bertram and William on the night of her arrival. (As before, Mrs. Stetson and Billy had gone directly to a hotel.) "I want a real home with a furnace to shake—if I want to—and some dirt to dig in."

"Well, I'm sure that ought to be easy to find," smiled Bertram.

"Oh, but that isn't all," supplemented Billy. "It must be mostly closets and piazza. At least, those are the important things."

"Well, you might run across a snag there. Why don't you build?"

Billy gave a gesture of dissent.

"Too slow. I want it now."

Bertram laughed. His eyes narrowed quizzically.

"From what Calderwell says," he bantered, "I should judge that there are plenty of sighing swains who are only too ready to give you a home—and now."

The pink deepened in Billy's cheeks.

"I said closets and a piazza, dirt to dig, and a furnace to shake," she retorted merrily. "I didn't say I wanted a husband."

"And you don't, of course," interposed William, decidedly. "You are much too young for that."

"Yes, sir," agreed Billy demurely; but Bertram was sure he saw a twinkle under the downcast lashes.

"And where is Cyril?" asked Mrs. Stetson, coming into the room at that moment.

William stirred restlessly.

"Well, Cyril couldn't—couldn't come," stammered William with an uneasy glance at his brother.

Billy laughed unexpectedly.

"It's too bad—about Mr. Cyril's not coming," she murmured. And again Bertram caught the twinkle in the downcast eyes.

To Bertram the twinkle looked interesting, and worth pursuit; but at the very beginning of the chase Calderwell's card came up, and that ended—everything, so Bertram declared crossly to himself.

Billy found her dirt to dig in, and her furnace to shake, in Brookline. There were closets, too, and a generous expanse of veranda. They all belonged to a quaint little house perched on the side of Corey Hill. From the veranda in the rear, and from many of the windows, one looked out upon a delightful view of many-hued, many-shaped roofs nestling among towering trees, with the wide sweep of the sky above, and the haze of faraway hills at the horizon.

"In fact, it's as nearly perfect as it can be—and not take angel-wings and fly away," declared Billy. "I have named it 'Hillside.'"

Very early in her career as house-owner, Billy decided that however delightful it might be to have a furnace to shake, it would not be at all delightful to shake it; besides, there was the new motor car to run. Billy therefore sought and found a good, strong man who had not only the muscle and the willingness to shake the furnace, but the skill to turn chauffeur at a moment's notice. Best of all, this man had also a wife who, with a maid to assist her, would take full charge of the house, and thus leave Billy and Mrs. Stetson free from care. All these, together with a canary, and a kitten as near like Spunk as could be obtained, made Billy's household.

"And now I'm ready to see my friends," she announced.

"And I think your friends will be ready to see you," Bertram assured her.

And they were—at least, so it appeared. For at once the little house perched on the hillside became the Mecca for many of the Henshaws' friends who had known Billy as William's merry, eighteen-year-old namesake. There were others, too, whom Billy had met abroad; and there were soft-stepping, sweet-faced old women and an occasional white-whiskered old man—Aunt Hannah's friends—who found that the young mistress of Hillside was a charming hostess. There were also the Henshaw "boys," and there was always Calderwell—at least, so Bertram declared to himself sometimes.

Bertram came frequently to the little house on the hill, even more frequently than William; but Cyril was not seen there so often. He came once at first, it is true, and followed Billy from room to room as she proudly displayed her new home. He showed polite interest in her view, and a perfunctory enjoyment of the tea she prepared for him. But he did not come again for some time, and when he did come, he sat stiffly silent, while his brothers did most of the talking.

As to Calderwell—Calderwell seemed suddenly to have lost his interest in impenetrable forests and unclimbable mountains. Nothing more intricate than the long Beacon Street boulevard, or more inaccessible than Corey Hill seemed worth exploring, apparently. According to Calderwell's own version of it, he had "settled down"; he was going to "be something that was something." And he did spend sundry of his morning hours in a Boston law office with ponderous, calf-bound volumes spread in imposing array on the desk before him. Other hours—many hours—he spent with Billy.

One day, very soon, in fact, after she arrived in Boston, Billy asked Calderwell about the Henshaws.

"Tell me about them," she said. "Tell me what they have been doing all these years."

"Tell you about them! Why, don't you know?"

She shook her head.

"No. Cyril says nothing. William little more—about themselves; and you know what Bertram is. One can hardly separate sense from nonsense with him."

"You don't know, then, how splendidly Bertram has done with his art?"

"No; only from the most casual hearsay. Has he done well then?"

"Finely! The public has been his for years, and now the critics are tumbling over each other to do him honor. They rave about his 'sensitive, brilliant, nervous touch,'—whatever that may be; his 'marvelous color sense'; his 'beauty of line and pose.' And they quarrel over whether it's realism or idealism that constitutes his charm."

"I'm so glad! And is it still the 'Face of a Girl'?"

"Yes; only he's doing straight portraiture now as well. It's got to be quite the thing to be 'done' by Henshaw; and there's many a fair lady that has graciously commissioned him to paint her portrait. He's a fine fellow, too—a mighty fine fellow. You may not know, perhaps, but three or four years ago he was—well, not wild, but 'frolicsome,' he would probably have called it. He got in with a lot of fellows that—well, that weren't good for a chap of Bertram's temperament."

"Like—Mr. Seaver?"

Calderwell turned sharply.

"Did YOU know Seaver?" he demanded in obvious surprise.

"I used to SEE him—with Bertram."

"Oh! Well, he WAS one of them, unfortunately. But Bertram shipped him years ago."

Billy gave a sudden radiant smile—but she changed the subject at once.

"And Mr. William still collects, I suppose," she observed.

"Jove! I should say he did! I've forgotten the latest; but he's a fine fellow, too, like Bertram."

"And—Mr. Cyril?"

Calderwell frowned.

"That chap's a poser for me, Billy, and no mistake. I can't make him out!"

"What's the matter?"

"I don't know. Probably I'm not 'tuned to his pitch.' Bertram told me once that Cyril was very sensitively strung, and never responded until a certain note was struck. Well, I haven't ever found that note, I reckon."

Billy laughed.

"I never heard Bertram say that, but I think I know what he means; and he's right, too. I begin to realize now what a jangling discord I must have created when I tried to harmonize with him three years ago! But what is he doing in his music?"

The other shrugged his shoulders.

"Same thing. Plays occasionally, and plays well, too; but he's so erratic it's difficult to get him to do it. Everything must be just so, you know—air, light, piano, and audience. He's got another book out, I'm told—a profound treatise on somebody's something or other—musical, of course."

"And he used to write music; doesn't he do that any more?"

"I believe so. I hear of it occasionally through musical friends of mine. They even play it to me sometimes. But I can't stand for much of it—his stuff—really, Billy."

"'Stuff' indeed! And why not?" An odd hostility showed in Billy's eyes.

Again Calderwell shrugged his shoulders.

"Don't ask me. I don't know. But they're always dead slow, somber things, with the wail of a lost spirit shrieking through them."

"But I just love lost spirits that wail," avowed Billy, with more than a shade of reproach in her voice.

Calderwell stared; then he shook his head.

"Not in mine, thank you;" he retorted whimsically. "I prefer my spirits of a more sane and cheerful sort."

The girl laughed, but almost instantly she fell silent.

"I've been wondering," she began musingly, after a time, "why some one of those three men does not—marry."

"You wouldn't wonder—if you knew them better," declared Calderwell. "Now think. Let's begin at the top of the Strata— by the way, Bertram's name for that establishment is mighty clever! First, Cyril: according to Bertram Cyril hates 'all kinds of women and other confusion'; and I fancy Bertram hits it about right. So that settles Cyril. Then there's William —you know William. Any girl would say William was a dear; but William isn't a MARRYING man. Dad says,"— Calderwell's voice softened a little—"dad says that William and his young wife were the most devoted couple that he ever saw; and that when she died she seemed to take with her the whole of William's heart—that is, what hadn't gone with the baby a few years before. There was a boy, you know, that died."

"Yes, I know," nodded Billy, quick tears in her eyes. "Aunt Hannah told me."

"Well, that counts out William, then," said Calderwell, with an air of finality.

"But how about Bertram? You haven't settled Bertram," laughed Billy, archly.

"Bertram!" Calderwell's eyes widened. "Billy, can you imagine Bertram's making love in real earnest to a girl?"

"Why, I—don't—know; maybe!" Billy tipped her head from side to side as if she were viewing a picture set up for her inspection.

"Well, I can't. In the first place, no girl would think he was serious; or if by any chance she did, she'd soon discover that it was the turn of her head or the tilt of her chin that he admired—TO PAINT. Now isn't that so?"

Billy laughed, but she did not answer.

"It is, and you know it," declared Calderwell. "And that settles him. Now you can see, perhaps, why none of these men—will marry."

It was a long minute before Billy spoke.

"Not a bit of it. I don't see it at all," she declared with roguish merriment. "Moreover, I think that some day, some one of them—will marry, Sir Doubtful!"

Calderwell threw a quick glance into her eyes. Evidently something he saw there sent a swift shadow to his own. He waited a moment, then asked abruptly:

"Billy, WON'T you marry me?"

Billy frowned, though her eyes still laughed.

"Hugh, I told you not to ask me that again," she demurred.

"And I told you not to ask impossibilities of me," he retorted imperturbably. "Billy, won't you, now—seriously?"

"Seriously, no, Hugh. Please don't let us go all over that again when we've done it so many times."

"No, let's don't," agreed the man, cheerfully. "And we don't have to, either, if you'll only say 'yes,' now right away, without any more fuss."

Billy sighed impatiently.

"Hugh, won't you understand that I'm serious?" she cried; then she turned suddenly, with a peculiar flash in her eyes.

"Hugh, I don't believe Bertram himself could make love any more nonsensically than you can!"

Calderwell laughed, but he frowned, too; and again he threw into Billy's face that keenly questioning glance. He said something—a light something—that brought the laugh to Billy's lips in spite of herself; but he was still frowning when he left the house some minutes later, and the shadow was not gone from his eyes.

CHAPTER XXIII

BERTRAM DOES SOME QUESTIONING

Billy's time was well occupied. There were so many, many things she wished to do, and so few, few hours in which to do them. First there was her music. She made arrangements at once to study with one of Boston's best piano teachers, and she also made plans to continue her French and German. She joined a musical club, a literary club, and a more strictly social club; and to numerous church charities and philanthropic enterprises she lent more than her name, giving freely of both time and money.

Friday afternoons, of course, were to be held sacred to the Symphony concerts; and on certain Wednesday mornings there was to be a series of recitals, in which she was greatly interested.

For Society with a capital S, Billy cared little; but for sociability with a small s, she cared much; and very wide she opened her doors to her friends, lavishing upon them a wealth of hospitality. Nor did they all come in carriages or automobiles—these friends. A certain pale-faced little widow over at the South End knew just how good Miss Neilson's tea tasted on a crisp October afternoon and Marie Hawthorn, a frail young woman who gave music lessons, knew just how restful was Miss Neilson's couch after a weary day of long walks and fretful pupils.

"But how in the world do you discover them all—these forlorn specimens of humanity?" queried Bertram one evening, when he had found Billy entertaining a freckled-faced messenger-boy with a plate of ice cream and a big square of cake.

"Anywhere—everywhere," smiled Billy.

"Well, this last candidate for your favor, who has just gone—who's he?"

"I don't know, beyond that his name is 'Tom,' and that he likes ice cream."

"And you never saw him before?"

"Never."

"Humph! One wouldn't think it, to see his charming air of nonchalant accustomedness."

"Oh, but it doesn't take much to make a little fellow like that feel at home," laughed Billy.

"And are you in the habit of feeding every one who comes to your house, on ice cream and chocolate cake? I thought that stone doorstep of yours was looking a little worn."

"Not a bit of it," retorted Billy. "This little chap came with a message just as I was finishing dinner. The ice cream was particularly good to-night, and it occurred to me that he might like a taste; so I gave it to him."

Bertram raised his eyebrows quizzically.

"Very kind, of course; but—why ice cream?" he questioned. "I thought it was roast beef and boiled potatoes that was supposed to be handed out to gaunt-eyed hunger."

"It is," nodded Billy, "and that's why I think sometimes they'd like ice cream and chocolate frosting. Besides, to give sugar plums one doesn't have to unwind yards of red tape, or worry about 'pauperizing the poor.' To give red flannels and a ton of coal, one must be properly circumspect and consult records and city missionaries, of course; and that's why it's such a relief sometimes just to hand over a simple little sugar plum and see them smile."

For a minute Bertram was silent, then he asked abruptly:

"Billy, why did you leave the Strata?"

Billy was taken quite by surprise. A pink flush spread to her forehead, and her tongue stumbled at first over her reply.

"Why, I—it seemed—you—why, I left to go to Hampden Falls, to be sure. Don't you remember?" she finished gaily.

"Oh, yes, I remember THAT," conceded Bertram with disdainful emphasis. "But why did you go to Hampden Falls?"

"Why, it—it was the only place to go—that is, I WANTED to go there," she corrected hastily. "Didn't Aunt Hannah tell you that I—I was homesick to get back there?"

"Oh, yes, Aunt Hannah SAID that," observed the man; "but wasn't that homesickness a little—sudden?"

Billy blushed pink again.

"Why, maybe; but—well, homesickness is always more or less sudden; isn't it?" she parried.

Bertram laughed, but his eyes grew suddenly almost tender.

"See here, Billy, you can't bluff worth a cent," he declared. "You are much too refreshingly frank for that. Something was the trouble. Now what was it? Won't you tell me, please?"

Billy pouted. She hesitated and gazed anywhere but into the challenging eyes before her. Then very suddenly she looked straight into them.

"Very well, there WAS a reason for my leaving," she confessed a little breathlessly. "I—didn't want to—bother you any more—all of you."

"Bother us!"

"No. I found out. You couldn't paint; Mr. Cyril couldn't play or write; and—and everything was different because I was there. But I didn't blame you—no, no!" she assured him hastily. "It was only that I—found out."

"And may I ask HOW you obtained this most extraordinary information?" demanded Bertram, savagely.

Billy shook her head. Her round little chin looked suddenly square and determined.

"You may ask, but I shall not tell," she declared firmly.

If Bertram had known Billy just a little better he would have let the matter drop there; but he did not know Billy, so he asked:

"Was it anything I did—or said?"

The girl did not answer.

"Billy, was it?" Bertram's voice showed terror now.

Billy laughed unexpectedly.

"Do you think I'm going to say 'no' to a series of questions, and then give the whole thing away by my silence when you come to the right one?" she demanded merrily. "No, sir!"

"Well, anyhow, it wasn't I, then," sighed the man in relief; "for you just observed that you were not going to say 'no to a series of questions'—and that was the first one. So I've found out that much, anyhow," he concluded triumphantly.

The girl eyed him for a moment in silence; then she shook her head.

"I'm not going to be caught that way, either," she smiled. "You know—just what you did in the first place about it: nothing."

The man stirred restlessly and pondered. After a long pause he adopted new tactics. With a searching study of her face to note the slightest change, he enumerated:

"Was it Cyril, then? Will? Aunt Hannah? Kate? It couldn't have been Pete, or Dong Ling!"

Billy still smiled inscrutably. At no name had Bertram detected so much as the flicker of an eyelid; and with a glance half-admiring, half-chagrined, he fell back into his chair.

"I'll give it up. You've won," he acknowledged. "But, Billy," —his manner changed suddenly—"I wonder if you know just what a hole you left in the Strata when you went away."

"But I couldn't have—in the whole Strata," objected Billy. "I occupied only one stratum, and a stratum doesn't go up and down, you know, only across; and mine was the second floor."

Bertram gave a slow shake of his head.

"I know; but yours was a freak formation," he maintained gravely. "It DID go up and down. Honestly, Billy, we did care—lots. Will and I were inconsolable, and even Cyril played dirges for a week."

"Did he?" gurgled Billy, with sudden joyousness. "I'm so glad!"

"Thank you," murmured Bertram, disapprovingly. "We hadn't considered it a subject for exultation."

"What? Oh, I didn't mean that! That is—" she stopped helplessly.

"Oh, never mind about trying to explain," interposed Bertram. "I fancy the remedy would be worse than the disease, in this case."

"Nonsense! I only meant that I like to be missed— sometimes," retorted Billy, a little nettled.

"And you rejoice then to have me mope, Cyril play dirges,

and Will wander mournfully about the house with Spunkie in his arms! You should have seen William. If his forlornness did not bring tears to your eyes, the grace of the pink bow that lopped behind Spunkie's left ear would surely have brought a copious flow."

Billy laughed, but her eyes grew tender.

"Did Uncle William do—that?" she asked.

"He did—and he did more. Pete told me after a time that you had not left one thing in the house, anywhere; but one day, over behind William's most treasured Lowestoft, I found a small shell hairpin, and a flat brown silk button that I recognized as coming from one of your dresses."

"Oh!" said Billy, softly. "Dear Uncle William—and how good he was to me!"

CHAPTER XXIV

CYRIL, THE ENIGMA

Perhaps it was because Billy saw so little of Cyril that it was Cyril whom she wished particularly to see. William, Bertram, Calderwell—all her other friends came frequently to the little house on the hill, Billy told herself; only Cyril held aloof—and it was Cyril that she wanted.

Billy said that it was his music; that she wanted to hear him play, and that she wanted him to hear her. She felt grieved and chagrined. Not once since she had come had he seemed interested—really interested in her music. He had asked her, it is true, in a perfunctory way what she had done, and who her teachers had been. But all the while she was answering she had felt that he was not listening; that he did not care. And she cared so much! She knew now that all her practising through the long hard months of study, had been for Cyril. Every scale had been smoothed for his ears, and every phrase had been interpreted with his approbation in view. Across the wide waste of waters his face had shone like a star of promise, beckoning her on and on to heights unknown... And now she was here in Boston, but she could not even play the scale, nor interpret the phrase for the ear to which they had been so laboriously attuned; and Cyril's face, in the flesh, was no beckoning star of promise, but was a thing as cold and relentless as was the waste of waters across which it had shone in the past.

Billy did not understand it. She knew, it is true, of Cyril's reputed aversion to women in general and to noise; but she was neither women in general nor noise, she told herself indignantly. She was only the little maid, grown three years older, who had sat at his feet and adoringly listened to all that he had been pleased to say in the old days at the top of the Strata. And he had been kind then—very kind, Billy declared stoutly. He had been patient and interested, too, and he had seemed not only willing, but glad to teach her, while now—

Sometimes Billy thought she would ask him candidly what was the matter. But it was always the old, frank Billy that thought this; the impulsive Billy, that had gone up to Cyril's rooms years before and cheerfully announced that she had come to get acquainted. It was never the sensible, circumspect Billy that Aunt Hannah had for three years been shaping and coaxing into being. But even this Billy frowned rebelliously, and declared that sometime something should be said that would at least give him a chance to explain.

In all the weeks since Billy's purchase of Hillside, Cyril had been there only twice, and it was nearly Thanksgiving now. Billy had seen him once or twice, also, at the Beacon Street house, when she and Aunt Hannah had dined there; but on all these occasions he had been either the coldly reserved guest or the painfully punctilious host. Never had he been in the least approachable.

"He treats me exactly as he treated poor little Spunk that first night," Billy declared hotly to herself.

Only once since she came had Billy heard Cyril play, and

that was when she had shared the privilege with hundreds of others at a public concert. She had sat then entranced, with her eyes on the clean-cut handsome profile of the man who played with so sure a skill and power, yet without a note before him. Afterward she had met him face to face, and had tried to tell him how moved she was; but in her agitation, and because of a strange shyness that had suddenly come to her, she had ended only in stammering out some flippant banality that had brought to his face merely a bored smile of acknowledgment.

Twice she had asked him to play for her; but each time he had begged to be excused, courteously, but decidedly.

"It's no use to tease," Bertram had interposed once, with an airy wave of his hands. "This lion always did refuse to roar to order. If you really must hear him, you'll have to slip up-stairs and camp outside his door, waiting patiently for such crumbs as may fall from his table."

"Aren't your metaphors a little mixed?" questioned Cyril irritably.

"Yes, sir," acknowledged Bertram with unruffled temper, "but I don't mind if Billy doesn't. I only meant her to understand that she'd have to do as she used to do—listen outside your door."

Billy's cheeks reddened.

"But that is what I sha'n't do," she retorted with spirit. "And, moreover, I still have hopes that some day he'll play to me."

"Maybe," conceded Bertram, doubtfully; "if the stool and the piano and the pedals and the weather and his fingers and your ears and my watch are all just right—then he'll play."

"Nonsense!" scowled Cyril. "I'll play, of course, some day. But I'd rather not today." And there the matter had ended. Since then Billy had not asked him to play.

CHAPTER XXV

THE OLD ROOM—AND BILLY

Thanksgiving was to be a great day in the Henshaw family. The Henshaw brothers were to entertain. Billy and Aunt Hannah had been invited to dinner; and so joyously hospitable was William's invitation that it would have included the new kitten and the canary if Billy would have consented to bring them.

Once more Pete swept and garnished the house, and once more Dong Ling spoiled uncounted squares of chocolate trying to make the baffling fudge. Bertram said that the entire Strata was a-quiver. Not but that Billy and Aunt Hannah had visited there before, but that this was different. They were to come at noon this time. This visit was not to be a tantalizing little piece of stiffness an hour and a half long. It was to be a satisfying, whole-souled matter of half a day's comradeship, almost like old times. So once more the roses graced the rooms, and a flaring pink bow adorned Spunkie's fat neck; and once more Bertram placed his latest "Face of a Girl" in the best possible light. There was still a difference, however, for this time Cyril did not bring any music down to the piano, nor display anywhere a copy of his newest book.

The dinner was to be at three o'clock, but by special

invitation the guests were to arrive at twelve; and promptly at the appointed hour they came.

"There, this is something like," exulted Bertram, when the ladies, divested of their wraps, toasted their feet before the open fire in his den.

"Indeed it is, for now I've time to see everything—everything you've done since I've been gone," cried Billy, gazing eagerly about her.

"Hm-m; well, THAT wasn't what I meant," shrugged Bertram.

"Of course not; but it's what I meant," retorted Billy. "And there are other things, too. I expect there are half a dozen new 'Old Blues' and black basalts that I want to see; eh, Uncle William?" she finished, smiling into the eyes of the man who had been gazing at her with doting pride for the last five minutes.

"Ho! Will isn't on teapots now," quoth Bertram, before his brother had a chance to reply. "You might dangle the oldest 'Old Blue' that ever was before him now, and he'd pay scant attention if he happened at the same time to get his eyes on some old pewter chain with a green stone in it."

Billy laughed; but at the look of genuine distress that came into William's face, she sobered at once.

"Don't you let him tease you, Uncle William," she said quickly. "I'm sure pewter chains with green stones in them sound just awfully interesting, and I want to see them right away now. Come," she finished, springing to her feet, "take me up-stairs, please, and show them to me."

William shook his head and said, "No, no!" protesting that what he had were scarcely worth her attention; but even while he talked he rose to his feet and advanced half eagerly, half reluctantly, toward the door.

"Nonsense," said Billy, fondly, as she laid her hand on his arm. "I know they are very much worth seeing. Come!" And she led the way from the room. "Oh, oh!" she exclaimed a few moments later, as she stood before a small cabinet in one of William's rooms. "Oh, oh, how pretty!"

"Do you like them? I thought you would," triumphed William, quick joy driving away the anxious fear in his eyes. "You see, I—I thought of you when I got them—every one of them. I thought you'd like them. But I haven't very many, yet, of course. This is the latest one." And he tenderly lifted from its black velvet mat a curious silver necklace made of small, flat, chain-linked disks, heavily chased, and set at regular intervals with a strange, blue-green stone.

Billy hung above it enraptured.

"Oh, what a beauty! And this, I suppose, is Bertram's 'pewter chain'! 'Pewter,' indeed!" she scoffed. "Tell me, Uncle William, where did you get it?"

And uncle William told, happily, thirstily, drinking in Billy's evident interest with delight. There were, too, a quaintly-set ring and a cat's-eye brooch; and to each belonged a story which William was equally glad to tell. There were other treasures, also: buckles, rings, brooches, and necklaces, some of dull gold, some of equally dull silver; but all of odd design and curious workmanship, studded here and there with bits of red, green, yellow, blue, and flame-colored stones. Very learnedly then from William's lips fell the new vocabulary that had come to him with his latest treasures: chrysoprase, carnelian, girasol, onyx, plasma, sardonyx, lapis lazuli, tourmaline, chrysolite, hyacinth, and carbuncle.

"They are lovely, perfectly lovely!" breathed Billy, when the last chain had slipped through her fingers into William's hand. "I think they are the very nicest things you ever collected."

"So do I," agreed the man, emphatically. "And they are—different, too."

"They are," said Billy, "very—different." But she was not looking at the jewelry: her eyes were on a small shell hairpin and a brown silk button half hidden behind a Lowestoft teapot.

On the way down-stairs William stopped a moment at Billy's old rooms.

"I wish you were here now," he said wistfully. "They're all ready for you—these rooms."

"Oh, but why don't you use them?—such pretty rooms!" cried Billy, quickly.

William gave a gesture of dissent.

"We have no use for them; besides, they belong to you and Aunt Hannah. You left your imprint long ago, my dear—we should not feel at home in them."

"Oh, but you should! You mustn't feel like that!" objected Billy, hurriedly crossing the room to the window to hide a sudden nervousness that had assailed her. "And here's my piano, too, and open!" she finished gaily, dropping herself upon the piano stool and dashing into a brilliant mazourka.

Billy, like Cyril, had a way of working off her moods at her finger tips; and to-day the tripping notes and crashing chords told of a nervous excitement that was not all joy. From the doorway William watched her flying fingers with fond pride, and it was very reluctantly that he acceded to Pete's request to go down-stairs for a moment to settle a vexed question concerning the table decorations.

Billy, left alone, still played, but with a difference. The tripping notes slowed into a weird melody that rose and fell and lost itself in the exquisite harmony that had been born of the crashing chords. Billy was improvising now, and into her music had crept something of her old-time longing when she had come to that house a lonely, orphan girl, in search of a home. On and on she played; then with a discordant note, she suddenly rose from the piano. She was thinking of Kate, and wondering if, had Kate not "managed" the little room would still be home.

So swiftly did Billy cross to the door that the man on the stairs outside had not time to get quite out of sight. Billy did not see his face, however; she saw only a pair of gray-trousered legs disappearing around the curve of the landing above. She thought nothing of it until later when dinner was announced, and Cyril came down-stairs; then she saw that he, and he only, that afternoon wore trousers of that particular shade of gray.

The dinner was a great success. Even the chocolate fudge in the little cut glass bonbon dishes was perfect; and it was a question whether Pete or Dong Ling tried the harder to please.

After dinner the family gathered in the drawing-room and chatted pleasantly. Bertram displayed his prettiest and newest pictures, and Billy played and sung—bright, tuneful little things that she knew Aunt Hannah and Uncle William liked. If Cyril was pleased or displeased, he did not show it—but Billy had ceased to play for Cyril's ears. She told herself that she did not care; but she did wonder: was that Cyril on the stairs, and if so—what was he doing there?

CHAPTER XXVI

"MUSIC HATH CHARMS"

Two days after Thanksgiving Cyril called at Hillside.

"I've come to hear you play," he announced abruptly.

Billy's heart sung within her—but her temper rose. Did he think then that he had but to beckon and she would come—and at this late day, she asked herself. Aloud she said:

"Play? But this is 'so sudden'! Besides, you have heard me."

The man made a disdainful gesture.

"Not that. I mean play—really play. Billy, why haven't you played to me before?"

Billy's chin rose perceptibly.

"Why haven't you asked me?" she parried.

To Billy's surprise the man answered this with calm directness.

"Because Calderwell said that you were a dandy player, and I don't care for dandy players."

Billy laughed now.

"And how do you know I'm not a dandy player, Sir Impertinent?" she demanded.

"Because I've heard you—when you weren't."

"Thank you," murmured Billy.

Cyril shrugged his shoulders.

"Oh, you know very well what I mean," he defended. "I've heard you; that's all."

"When?"

"That doesn't signify."

Billy was silent for a moment, her eyes gravely studying his face. Then she asked:

"Were you long—on that stairway?"

"Eh? What? Oh!" Cyril's forehead grew suddenly pink. "Well?" he finished a little aggressively.

"Oh, nothing," smiled the girl. "Of course people who live in glass houses must not throw stones."

"Very well then, I did listen," acknowledged the man, testily. "I liked what you were playing. I hoped, down-stairs later, that you'd play it again; but you didn't. I came to-day to hear it."

Again Billy's heart sung within her—but again her temper rose, too.

"I don't think I feel like it," she said sweetly, with a shake of her head. "Not to-day."

For a brief moment Cyril stared frowningly; then his face lighted with his rare smile.

"I'm fairly checkmated," he said, rising to his feet and going straight to the piano.

For long minutes he played, modulating from one enchanting composition to another, and finishing with the one "all chords with big bass notes" that marched on and on—the one Billy had sat long ago on the stairs to hear.

"There! Now will you play for me?" he asked, rising to his feet, and turning reproachful eyes upon her.

Billy, too, rose to her feet. Her face was flushed and her eyes were shining. Her lips quivered with emotion. As was always the case, Cyril's music had carried her quite out of herself.

"Oh, thank you, thank you," she sighed. "You don't know— you can't know how beautiful it all is—to me!"

"Thank you. Then surely now you'll play to me," he returned.

A look of real distress came to Billy's face.

"But I can't—not what you heard the other day," she cried remorsefully. "You see, I was—only improvising."

Cyril turned quickly.

Eleanor H. Porter

"Only improvising! Billy, did you ever write it down—any of your improvising?"

An embarrassed red flew to Billy's face.

"Not—not that amounted to—well, that is, some—a little," she stammered.

"Let me see it."

"No, no, I couldn't—not YOU!"

Again the rare smile lighted Cyril's eyes.

"Billy, let me see that paper—please."

Very slowly the girl turned toward the music cabinet. She hesitated, glanced once more appealingly into Cyril's face, then with nervous haste opened the little mahogany door and took from one of the shelves a sheet of manuscript music. But, like a shy child with her first copy book, she held it half behind her back as she came toward the piano.

"Thank you," said Cyril as he reached far out for the music. The next moment he seated himself again at the piano.

Twice he played the little song through carefully, slowly.

"Now, sing it," he directed.

Falteringly, in a very faint voice, and with very many breaths taken where they should not have been taken, Billy obeyed.

"When we want to show off your song, Billy, we won't ask you to sing it," observed the man, dryly, when she had finished.

Billy laughed and dimpled into a blush.

"When I want to show off my song I sha'n't be singing it to you for the first time," she pouted.

Cyril did not answer. He was playing over and over certain harmonies in the music before him.

"Hm-m; I see you've studied your counterpoint to some purpose," he vouchsafed, finally; then: "Where did you get the words?"

The girl hesitated. The flush had deepened on her face.

"Well, I—" she stopped and gave an embarrassed laugh. "I'm like the small boy who made the toys. 'I got them all out of my own head, and there's wood enough to make another.'"

"Hm-m; indeed!" grunted the man. "Well, have you made any others?"

"One—or two, maybe."

"Let me see them, please."

"I think—we've had enough—for today," she faltered.

"I haven't. Besides, if I could have a couple more to go with this, it would make a very pretty little group of songs."

"'To go with this'! What do you mean?"

"To the publishers, of course."

"The PUBLISHERS!"

"Certainly. Did you think you were going to keep these songs to yourself?"

"But they aren't worth it! They can't be—good enough!" Unbelieving joy was in Billy's voice.

"No? Well, we'll let others decide that," observed Cyril, with a shrug. "All is, if you've got any more wood—like this—I advise you to make it up right away."

"But I have already!" cried the girl, excitedly. "There are lots of little things that I've—that is, there are—some," she corrected hastily, at the look that sprang into Cyril's eyes.

"Oh, there are," laughed Cyril. "Well, we'll see what—" But he did not see. He did not even finish his sentence; for Billy's maid, Rosa, appeared just then with a card.

"Show Mr. Calderwell in here," said Billy. Cyril said nothing —aloud; which was well. His thoughts, just then, were better left unspoken.

CHAPTER XXVII

MARIE, WHO LONGS TO MAKE PUDDINGS

Wonderful days came then to Billy. Four songs, it seemed, had been pronounced by competent critics decidedly "worth it"—unmistakably "good enough"; and they were to be brought out as soon as possible.

"Of course you understand," explained Cyril, "that there's no 'hit' expected. Thank heaven they aren't that sort! And there's no great money in it, either. You'd have to write a masterpiece like 'She's my Ju-Ju Baby' or some such gem to get the 'hit' and the money. But the songs are fine, and they'll take with cultured hearers. We'll get them introduced by good singers, of course, and they'll be favorites soon for the concert stage, and for parlors."

Billy saw a good deal of Cyril now. Already she was at work rewriting and polishing some of her half-completed melodies, and Cyril was helping her, by his interest as well as by his criticism. He was, in fact, at the house very frequently— too frequently, indeed, to suit either Bertram or Calderwell. Even William frowned sometimes when his cozy chats with Billy were interrupted by Cyril's appearing with a roll of new music for her to "try"; though William told himself that he ought to be thankful if there was anything that could make

Eleanor H. Porter

Cyril more companionable, less reserved and morose. And Cyril WAS different—there was no disputing that. Calderwell said that he had come "out of his shell"; and Bertram told Billy that she must have "found his note and struck it good and hard."

Billy was very happy. To the little music teacher, Marie Hawthorn, she talked more freely, perhaps, than she did to any one else.

"It's so wonderful, Marie—so wonderfully wonderful," she said one day, "to sit here in my own room and sing a little song that comes from somewhere, anywhere, out of the sky itself. Then by and by, that little song will fly away, away, over land and sea; and some day it will touch somebody's heart just as it has touched mine. Oh, Marie, is it not wonderful?"

"It is, dear—and it is not. Your songs could not help reaching somebody's heart. There's nothing wonderful in that."

"Sweet flatterer!"

"But I mean it. They are beautiful; and so is—Mr. Henshaw's music."

"Yes, it is," murmured Billy, abstractedly.

There was a long pause, then Marie asked with shy hesitation:

"Do you think, Miss Billy—that he would care? I listened yesterday when he was playing to you. I was up here in your room, but when I heard the music I—I went out, on the stairs and sat down. Was it very—bad of me?"

Billy laughed happily.

"If it was, he can't say anything," she reassured her. "He's done the same thing himself—and so have I."

"HE has done it!"

"Yes. It was at his home last Thanksgiving. It was then that he found out—about my improvising."

"Oh-h!" Marie's eyes were wistful. "And he cares so much now for your music!"

"Does he? Do you think he does?" demanded Billy.

"I know he does—and for the one who makes it, too."

"Nonsense!" laughed Billy, with pinker cheeks. "It's the music, not the musician, that pleases him. Mr. Cyril doesn't like women."

"He doesn't like women!"

"No. But don't look so shocked, my dear. Every one who knows Mr. Cyril knows that."

"But I don't think—I believe it," demurred Marie, gazing straight into Billy's eyes. "I'm sure I don't believe it."

Under the little music teacher's steady gaze Billy flushed again. The laugh she gave was an embarrassed one, but through it vibrated a pleased ring.

"Nonsense!" she exclaimed, springing to her feet and moving restlessly about the room. With the next breath she had changed the subject to one far removed from Mr. Cyril and his likes and dislikes.

Some time later Billy played, and it was then that Marie drew a long sigh.

"How beautiful it must be to play—like that," she breathed.

"As if you, a music teacher, could not play!" laughed Billy.

"Not like that, dear. You know it is not like that."

Billy frowned.

"But you are so accurate, Marie, and you can read at sight so rapidly!"

"Oh, yes, like a little machine, I know!" scorned the usually gentle Marie, bitterly. "Don't they have a thing of metal that adds figures like magic? Well, I'm like that. I see g and I play g; I see d and I play d; I see f and I play f; and after I've seen enough g's and d's and f's and played them all, the thing is done. I've played."

"Why, Marie! Marie, my dear!" The second exclamation was very tender, for Marie was crying.

"There! I knew I should some day have it out—all out," sobbed Marie. "I felt it coming."

"Then perhaps you'll—you'll feel better now," stammered Billy. She tried to say more—other words that would have been a real comfort; but her tongue refused to speak them. She knew so well, so woefully well, how very wooden and mechanical the little music teacher's playing always had been. But that Marie should realize it herself like this—the tragedy of it made Billy's heart ache. At Marie's next words, however, Billy caught her breath in surprise.

"But you see it wasn't music—it wasn't ever music that I wanted—to do," she confessed.

"It wasn't music! But what—I don't understand," murmured Billy.

"No, I suppose not," sighed the other. "You play so beautifully yourself."

"But I thought you loved music."

"I do. I love it dearly—in others. But I can't—I don't want to make it myself."

"But what do you want to do?"

Marie laughed suddenly.

"Do you know, my dear, I have half a mind to tell you what I do like to do—just to make you stare."

"Well?" Billy's eyes were wide with interest.

"I like best of anything to—darn stockings and make puddings."

"Marie!"

"Rank heresy, isn't it?" smiled Marie, tearfully. "But I do, truly. I love to weave the threads evenly in and out, and see a big hole close. As for the puddings I don't mean the common bread-and-butter kind, but the ones that have whites of eggs and fruit, and pretty quivery jellies all ruby and amber lights, you know."

"You dear little piece of domesticity," laughed Billy. "Then why in the world don't you do these things?"

"I can't, in my own kitchen; I can't afford a kitchen to do them in. And I just couldn't do them—right along—in other people's kitchens."

"But why do you—play?"

"I was brought up to it. You know we had money once, lots of it," sighed Marie, as if she were deploring a misfortune. "And mother was determined to have me musical. Even then, as a little tot, I liked pudding-making, and after my mud-pie days I was always begging mother to let me go down into the kitchen, to cook. But she wouldn't allow it, ever. She engaged the most expensive masters and set me practising, always practising. I simply had to learn music; and I learned it like the adding machine. Then afterward, when father died, and then mother, and the money flew away, why, of course I had to do something, so naturally I turned to the music. It was all I could do. But—well, you know how it is, dear. I teach, and teach well, perhaps, so far as the mechanical part goes; but as for the rest—I am always longing for a cozy corner with a basket of stockings to mend, or a kitchen where there is a pudding waiting to be made."

"You poor dear!" cried Billy. "I've a pair of stockings now that needs attention, and I've been just longing for one of your 'quivery jellies all ruby and amber lights' ever since you mentioned them. But—well, is there anything I could do to help?"

"Nothing, thank you," sighed Marie, rising wearily to her feet, and covering her eyes with her hand for a moment. "My head aches shockingly, but I've got to go this minute and instruct little Jennie Knowls how to play the wonderful scale of G with a black key in it. Besides, you do help me, you have helped me, you are always helping me, dear," she added remorsefully; "and it's wicked of me to make that shadow come to your eyes. Please don't think of it, or of me, any more." And with a choking little sob she hurried from the room, followed by the amazed, questioning, sorrowful eyes of Billy.

CHAPTER XXVIII

"I'M GOING TO WIN"

Nearly all of Billy's friends knew that Bertram Henshaw was in love with Billy Neilson before Billy herself knew it. Not that they regarded it as anything serious—"it's only Bertram" was still said of him on almost all occasions. But to Bertram himself it was very serious.

The world to Bertram, indeed, had come to assume a vastly different aspect from what it had displayed in times past. Heretofore it had been a plaything which like a juggler's tinsel ball might be tossed from hand to hand at will. Now it was no plaything—no glittering bauble. It was something big and serious and splendid—because Billy lived in it; something that demanded all his powers to do, and be—because Billy was watching; something that might be a Hades of torment or an Elysium of bliss—according to whether Billy said "no" or "yes."

Since Thanksgiving Bertram had known that it was love—this consuming fire within him; and since Thanksgiving he had known, too, that it was jealousy—this fierce hatred of Calderwell. He was ashamed of the hatred. He told himself that it was unmanly, unkind, and unreasonable; and he vowed that he would overcome it. At times he even fancied that he had overcome it; but always the sight of Calderwell in Billy's little drawing-room or of even the man's card on Billy's silver tray was enough to show him that he had not.

There were others, too, who annoyed Bertram not a little, foremost of these being his own brothers. Still he was not really worried about William and Cyril, he told himself. William he did not consider to be a marrying man; and Cyril—every one knew that Cyril was a woman-hater. He was doubtless attracted now only by Billy's music. There was no real rivalry to be feared from William and Cyril. But there was always Calderwell, and Calderwell was serious. Bertram decided, therefore, after some weeks of feverish unrest, that the only road to peace lay through a frank avowal of his feelings, and a direct appeal to Billy to give him the great boon of her love.

Just here, however, Bertram met with an unexpected difficulty. He could not find words with which to make his avowal or to present his appeal. He was surprised and annoyed. Never before had he been at a loss for words— mere words. And it was not that he lacked opportunity. He walked, drove, and talked with Billy, and always she was companionable, attentive to what he had to say. Never was she cold or reserved. Never did she fail to greet him with a cheery smile.

Bertram concluded, indeed, after a time, that she was too companionable, too cheery. He wished she would hesitate, stammer, blush; be a little shy. He wished that she would display surprise, annoyance, even—anything but that eternal air of comradeship. And then, one afternoon in the early twilight of a January day, he freed his mind, quite unexpectedly.

"Billy, I wish you WOULDN'T be so—so friendly!" he

exclaimed in a voice that was almost sharp.

Billy laughed at first, but the next moment a shamed distress drove the merriment quite out of her face.

"You mean that I presume on—on our friendship?" she stammered. "That you fear that I will again—shadow your footsteps?" It was the first time since the memorable night itself that Billy had ever in Bertram's presence referred to her young guardianship of his welfare. She realized now, suddenly, that she had just been giving the man before her some very "sisterly advice," and the thought sent a confused red to her cheeks.

Bertram turned quickly.

"Billy, that was the dearest and loveliest thing a girl ever did—only I was too great a chump to appreciate it!" finished Bertram in a voice that was not quite steady.

"Thank you," smiled the girl, with a slow shake of her head and a relieved look in her eyes; "but I'm afraid I can't quite agree to that." The next moment she had demanded mischievously: "Why, then, pray, this unflattering objection to my—friendliness now?"

"Because I don't want you for a friend, or a sister, or anything else that's related," stormed Bertram, with sudden vehemence. "I don't want you for anything but—a wife! Billy, WON'T you marry me?"

Again Billy laughed—laughed until she saw the pained anger leap to the gray eyes before her; then she became grave at once.

"Bertram, forgive me. I didn't think you could—you can't

be—serious!"

"But I am."

Billy shook her head.

"But you don't love me—not ME, Bertram. It's only the turn of my head or—or the tilt of my chin that you love—to paint," she protested, unconsciously echoing the words Calderwell had said to her weeks before. "I'm only another 'Face of a Girl.'"

"You're the only 'Face of a girl' to me now, Billy," declared the man, with disarming tenderness.

"No, no, not that," demurred Billy, in distress. "You don't mean it. You only think you do. It couldn't be that. It can't be!"

"But it is, dear. I think I have loved you ever since that night long ago when I saw your dear, startled face appealing to me from beyond Seaver's hateful smile. And, Billy, I never went once with Seaver again—anywhere. Did you know that?"

"No; but—I'm glad—so glad!"

"And I'm glad, too. So you see, I must have loved you then, though unconsciously, perhaps; and I love you now."

"No, no, please don't say that. It can't be—it really can't be. I—I don't love you—that way, Bertram."

The man paled a little.

"Billy—forgive me for asking, but it's so much to me—is it that there is—some one else?" His voice shook.

"No, no, indeed! There is no one."

"It's not—Calderwell?"

Billy's forehead grew pink. She laughed nervously.

"No, no, never!"

"But there are others, so many others!"

"Nonsense, Bertram; there's no one—no one, I assure you!"

"It's not William, of course, nor Cyril. Cyril hates women."

A deeper flush came to Billy's face. Her chin rose a little; and an odd defiance flashed from her eyes. But almost instantly it was gone, and a slow smile had come to her lips.

"Yes, I know. Every one—says that Cyril hates women," she observed demurely.

"Then, Billy, I sha'n't give up!" vowed Bertram, softly. "Sometime you WILL love me!"

"No, no, I couldn't. That is, I'm not going to—to marry," stammered Billy.

"Not going to marry!"

"No. There's my music—you know how I love that, and how much it is to me. I don't think there'll ever be a man—that I'll love better."

Bertram lifted his head. Very slowly he rose till his splendid six feet of clean-limbed strength and manly beauty towered away above the low chair in which Billy sat. His mouth showed new lines about the corners, and his eyes looked down very tenderly at the girl beside him; but his voice, when he spoke, had a light whimsicality that deceived even Billy's ears.

"And so it's music—a cold, senseless thing of spidery marks on clean white paper—that is my only rival," he cried. "Then I'll warn you, Billy, I'll warn you. I'm going to win!" And with that he was gone.

CHAPTER XXIX

"I'M NOT GOING TO MARRY"

Billy did not know whether to be more amazed or amused at Bertram's proposal of marriage. She was vexed; she was very sure of that. To marry Bertram? Absurd!... Then she reflected that, after all, it was only Bertram, so she calmed herself.

Still, it was annoying. She liked Bertram, she had always liked him. He was a nice boy, and a most congenial companion. He never bored her, as did some others; and he was always thoughtful of cushions and footstools and cups of tea when one was tired. He was, in fact, an ideal friend, just the sort she wanted; and it was such a pity that he must spoil it all now with this silly sentimentality! And of course he had spoiled it all. There was no going back now to their old friendliness. He would be morose or silly by turns, according to whether she frowned or smiled; or else he would take himself off in a tragic sort of way that was very disturbing. He had said, to be sure, that he would "win." Win, indeed! As if she could marry Bertram! When she married, her choice would fall upon a man, not a boy; a big, grave, earnest man to whom the world meant something; a man who loved music, of course; a man who would single her out from all the world, and show to her, and to her only, the depth and tenderness of his love; a man who—but she was not going to marry, anyway, remembered Billy, suddenly. And with that she began to cry. The whole thing was so "tiresome," she declared, and so "absurd."

Billy rather dreaded her next meeting with Bertram. She feared—she knew not what. But, as it turned out, she need not have feared anything, for he met her tranquilly, cheerfully, as usual; and he did nothing and said nothing that he might not have done and said before that twilight chat took place.

Billy was relieved. She concluded that, after all, Bertram was going to be sensible. She decided that she, too, would be sensible. She would accept him on this, his chosen plane, and she would think no more of his "nonsense."

Billy threw herself then even more enthusiastically into her beloved work. She told Marie that after all was said and done, there could not be any man that would tip the scales one inch with music on the other side. She was a little hurt, it is true, when Marie only laughed and answered:

"But what if the man and the music both happen to be on the same side, my dear; what then?"

Marie's voice was wistful, in spite of the laugh—so wistful that it reminded Billy of their conversation a few weeks before.

"But it is you, Marie, who want the stockings to darn and the puddings to make," she retorted playfully. "Not I! And, do you know? I believe I shall turn matchmaker yet, and find you a man; and the chiefest of his qualifications shall be that he's wretchedly hard on his hose, and that he adores puddings."

"No, no, Miss Billy, don't, please!" begged the other, in quick terror. "Forget all I said the other day; please do! Don't tell—anybody!"

She was so obviously distressed and frightened that Billy was puzzled.

"There, there, 'twas only a jest, of course," she soothed her. "But, really Marie, it is the dear, domestic little mouse like yourself that ought to be somebody's wife—and that's the kind men are looking for, too."

Marie gave a slow shake of her head.

"Not the kind of man that is somebody, that does something," she objected; "and that's the only kind I could—love. HE wants a wife that is beautiful and clever, that can do things like himself—LIKE HIMSELF!" she iterated feverishly.

Billy opened wide her eyes.

"Why, Marie, one would think—you already knew—such a man," she cried.

The little music teacher changed her position, and turned her eyes away.

"I do, of course," she retorted in a merry voice, "lots of them. Don't you? Come, we've discussed my matrimonial prospects quite long enough," she went on lightly. "You know we started with yours. Suppose we go back to those."

"But I haven't any," demurred Billy, as she turned with a smile to greet Aunt Hannah, who had just entered the room. "I'm not going to marry; am I, Aunt Hannah?"

"Er—what? Marry? My grief and conscience, what a question, Billy! Of course you're going to marry—when the time comes!" exclaimed Aunt Hannah.

Billy laughed and shook her head vigorously. But even as she opened her lips to reply, Rosa appeared and announced that Mr. Calderwell was waiting down-stairs. Billy was angry then, for after the maid was gone, the merriment in Aunt Hannah's laugh only matched that in Marie's—and the intonation was unmistakable.

"Well, I'm not!" declared Billy with pink cheeks and much indignation, as she left the room. And as if to convince herself, Marie, Aunt Hannah, and all the world that such was the case, she refused Calderwell so decidedly that night when he, for the half-dozenth time, laid his hand and heart at her feet, that even Calderwell himself was convinced—so far as his own case was concerned—and left town the next day.

Bertram told Aunt Hannah afterward that he understood Mr. Calderwell had gone to parts unknown. To himself Bertram shamelessly owned that the more "unknown" they were, the better he himself would be pleased.

CHAPTER XXX

MARIE FINDS A FRIEND

It was on a very cold January afternoon, and Cyril was hurrying up the hill toward Billy's house, when he was startled to see a slender young woman sitting on a curbstone with her head against an electric-light post. He stopped abruptly.

"I beg your pardon, but—why, Miss Hawthorn! It is Miss Hawthorn; isn't it?"

Under his questioning eyes the girl's pale face became so painfully scarlet that in sheer pity the man turned his eyes away. He thought he had seen women blush before, but he decided now that he had not.

"I'm sure—haven't I met you at Miss Neilson's? Are you ill? Can't I do something for you?" he begged.

"Yes—no—that is, I AM Miss Hawthorn, and I've met you at Miss Neilson's," stammered the girl, faintly. "But there isn't anything, thank you, that you can do—Mr. Henshaw. I stopped to rest."

The man frowned.

"But, surely—pardon me, Miss Hawthorn, but I can't think it your usual custom to choose an icy curbstone for a resting place, with the thermometer down to zero. You must be ill. Let me take you to Miss Neilson's."

"No, no, thank you," cried the girl, struggling to her feet, the vivid red again flooding her face. "I have a lesson—to give."

"Nonsense! You're not fit to give a lesson. Besides, they are all folderol, anyway, half of them. A dozen lessons, more or less, won't make any difference; they'll play just as well—and just as atrociously. Come, I insist upon taking you to Miss Neilson's."

"No, no, thank you! I really mustn't. I—" She could say no more. A strong, yet very gentle hand had taken firm hold of her arm in such a way as half to support her. A force quite outside of herself was carrying her forward step by step—and Miss Hawthorn was not used to strong, gentle hands, nor yet to a force quite outside of herself. Neither was she accustomed to walk arm in arm with Mr. Cyril Henshaw to Miss Billy's door. When she reached there her cheeks were like red roses for color, and her eyes were like the stars for brightness. Yet a minute later, confronted by Miss Billy's astonished eyes, the stars and the roses fled, and a very white-faced girl fell over in a deathlike faint in Cyril Henshaw's arms.

Marie was put to bed in the little room next to Billy's, and was peremptorily hushed when faint remonstrance was made. The next morning, white-faced and wide-eyed, she resolutely pulled herself half upright, and announced that she was all well and must go home—home to Marie was a six-by-nine hall bed-room in a South End lodging house.

Very gently Billy pushed her back on the pillow and laid a

detaining hand on her arm.

"No, dear. Now, please be sensible and listen to reason. You are my guest. You did not know it, perhaps, for I'm afraid the invitation got a little delayed. But you're to stay—oh, lots of weeks."

"I—stay here? Why, I can't—indeed, I can't," protested Marie.

"But that isn't a bit of a nice way to accept an invitation," disapproved Billy. "You should say, 'Thank you, I'd be delighted, I'm sure, and I'll stay.'"

In spite of herself the little music teacher laughed, and in the laugh her tense muscles relaxed.

"Miss Billy, Miss Billy, what is one to do with you? Surely you know—you must know that I can't do what you ask!"

"I'm sure I don't see why not," argued Billy. "I'm merely giving you an invitation and all you have to do is to accept it."

"But the invitation is only the kind way your heart has of covering another of your many charities," objected Marie; "besides, I have to teach. I have my living to earn."

"But you can't," demurred the other. "That's just the trouble. Don't you see? The doctor said last night that you must not teach again this winter."

"Not teach—again—this winter! No, no, he could not be so cruel as that!"

"It wasn't cruel, dear; it was kind. You would be ill if you attempted it. Now you'll get better. He says all you need is rest and care—and that's exactly what I mean my guest shall have."

Quick tears came to the sick girl's eyes.

"There couldn't be a kinder heart than yours, Miss Billy," she murmured, "but I couldn't—I really couldn't be a burden to you like this. I shall go to some hospital."

"But you aren't going to be a burden. You are going to be my friend and companion."

"A companion—and in bed like this?"

"Well, THAT wouldn't be impossible," smiled Billy; "but, as it happens you won't have to put that to the test, for you'll soon be up and dressed. The doctor says so. Now surely you will stay."

There was a long pause. The little music teacher's eyes had left Billy's face and were circling the room, wistfully lingering on the hangings of filmy lace, the dainty wall covering, and the exquisite water colors in their white-and-gold frames. At last she drew a deep sigh.

"Yes, I'll stay," she breathed rapturously; "but—you must let me help."

"Help? Help what?"

"Help you; your letters, your music-copying, your accounts —anything, everything. And if you don't let me help,"—the music teacher's voice was very stern now—"if you don't let me help, I shall go home just—as—soon—as—I—can—walk!"

Eleanor H. Porter

"Dear me!" dimpled Billy. "And is that all? Well, you shall help, and to your heart's content, too. In fact, I'm not at all sure that I sha'n't keep you darning stockings and making puddings all the time," she added mischievously, as she left the room.

Miss Hawthorn sat up the next day. The day following, in one of Billy's "fluttery wrappers," as she called them, she walked all about the room. Very soon she was able to go down-stairs, and in an astonishingly short time she fitted into the daily life as if she had always been there. She was, moreover, of such assistance to Billy that even she herself could see the value of her work; and so she stayed, content.

The little music teacher saw a good deal of Billy's friends then, particularly of the Henshaw brothers; and very glad was Billy to see the comradeship growing between them. She had known that William would be kind to the orphan girl, but she had feared that Marie would not understand Bertram's nonsense or Cyril's reserve. But very soon Bertram had begged, and obtained, permission to try to reproduce on canvas the sheen of the fine, fair hair, and the veiled bloom of the rose-leaf skin that were Marie's greatest charms; and already Cyril had unbent from his usual stiffness enough to play to her twice. So Billy's fears on that score were at an end.

CHAPTER XXXI

THE ENGAGEMENT OF ONE

Many times during those winter days Billy thought of Marie's words: "But what if the man and the music both happen to be on the same side?" They worried her, to some extent, and, curiously, they pleased and displeased her at the same time.

She told herself that she knew very well, of course, what Marie meant: it was Cyril; he was the man, and the music. But was Cyril beginning to care for her; and did she want him to? Very seriously one day Billy asked herself these questions; very calmly she argued the matter in her mind—as was Billy's way.

She was proud, certainly, of what her influence had apparently done for Cyril. She was gratified that to her he was showing the real depth and beauty of his nature. It WAS flattering to feel that she, and only she, had thus won the regard of a professional woman-hater. Then, besides all this, there was his music—his glorious music. Think of the bliss of living ever with that! Imagine life with a man whose soul would be so perfectly attuned to hers that existence would be one grand harmony! Ah, that, truly, would be the ideal marriage! But she had planned not to marry. Billy frowned now, and tapped her foot nervously. It was, indeed, most puzzling—this question, and she did not want to make a mistake. Then, too, she did not wish to wound Cyril. If the dear man HAD come out of his icy prison, and were reaching out timid hands to her for her help, her interest, her love—the tragedy of it, if he met with no response!.... This vision of Cyril with outstretched hands, and of herself with cold, averted eyes was the last straw in the balance with Billy. She decided suddenly that she did care for Cyril—a little; and that she probably could care for him a great deal. With this thought, Billy blushed—already in her own mind she was as good as pledged to Cyril.

It was a great change for Billy—this sudden leap from girlhood and irresponsibility to womanhood and care; but she took it fearlessly, resolutely. If she was to be Cyril's wife she must make herself fit for it—and in pursuance of this high ideal she followed Marie into the kitchen the very next time the little music teacher went out to make one of her dainty desserts that the family liked so well.

"I'll just watch, if you don't mind," announced Billy.

"Why, of course not," smiled Marie, "but I thought you didn't like to make puddings."

"I don't," owned Billy, cheerfully.

"Then why this watchfulness?"

"Nothing, only I thought it might be just as well if I knew how to make them. You know how Cyril—that is, ALL the Henshaw boys like every kind you make."

The egg in Marie's hand slipped from her fingers and crashed untidily on the shelf. With a gleeful laugh Billy welcomed the diversion. She had not meant to speak so plainly. It was one thing to try to fit herself to be Cyril's wife, and quite another to display those efforts so openly before the world.

The pudding was made at last, but Marie proved to be a nervous teacher. Her hand shook, and her memory almost failed her at one or two critical points. Billy laughingly said that it must be stage fright, owing to the presence of herself as spectator; and with this Marie promptly, and somewhat effusively, agreed.

So very busy was Billy during the next few days, acquiring her new domesticity, that she did not notice how little she was seeing of Cyril. Then she suddenly realized it, and asked herself the reason for it. Cyril was at the house certainly, just as frequently as he had been; but she saw that a new shyness in herself had developed which was causing her to be restless in his presence, and was leading her to like better to have Marie or Aunt Hannah in the room when he called. She discovered, too, that she welcomed William, and even Bertram, with peculiar enthusiasm—if they happened to interrupt a tete-a-tete with Cyril.

Billy was disturbed at this. She told herself that this shyness was not strange, perhaps, inasmuch as her ideas in regard to love and marriage had undergone so abrupt a change; but it must be overcome. If she was to be Cyril's wife, she must like to be with him—and of course she really did like to be with him, for she had enjoyed his companionship very much during all these past weeks. She set herself therefore, now, determinedly to cultivating Cyril.

It was then that Billy made a strange and fearsome discovery: there were some things about Cyril that she did—not—like!

Eleanor H. Porter

Billy was inexpressibly shocked. Heretofore he had been so high, so irreproachable, so god-like!—but heretofore he had been a friend. Now he was appearing in a new role—though unconsciously, she knew. Heretofore she had looked at him with eyes that saw only the delightful and marvelous unfolding of a coldly reserved nature under the warmth of her own encouraging smile. Now she looked at him with eyes that saw only the possibilities of that same nature when it should have been unfolded in a lifelong companionship. And what she saw frightened her. There was still the music—she acknowledged that; but it had come to Billy with overwhelming force that music, after all, was not everything. The man counted, as well. Very frankly then Billy stated the case to herself.

"What passes for 'fascinating mystery' in him now will be plain moroseness—sometime. He is 'taciturn' now; he'll be— cross, then. It is 'erratic' when he won't play the piano to-day; but a few years from now, when he refuses some simple request of mine, it will be—stubbornness. All this it will be —if I don't love him; and I don't. I know I don't. Besides, we aren't really congenial. I like people around; he doesn't. I like to go to plays; he doesn't. He likes rainy days; I abhor them. There is no doubt of it—life with him would not be one grand harmony; it would be one jangling discord. I simply cannot marry him. I shall have to break the engagement!"

Billy spoke with regretful sorrow. It was evident that she grieved to bring pain to Cyril. Then suddenly the gloom left her face: she had remembered that the "engagement" was just three weeks old—and was a profound secret, not only to the bridegroom elect, but to all the world as well—save herself!

Billy was very happy after that. She sang about the house all day, and she danced sometimes from room to room, so light were her feet and her heart. She made no more puddings with Marie's supervision, but she was particularly careful to have the little music teacher or Aunt Hannah with her when Cyril called. She made up her mind, it is true, that she had been mistaken, and that Cyril did not love her; still she wished to be on the safe side, and she became more and more averse to being left alone with him for any length of time.

CHAPTER XXXII

CYRIL HAS SOMETHING TO SAY

Long before spring Billy was forced to own to herself that her fancied security from lovemaking on the part of Cyril no longer existed. She began to suspect that there was reason for her fears. Cyril certainly was "different." He was more approachable, less reserved, even with Marie and Aunt Hannah. He was not nearly so taciturn, either, and he was much more gracious about his playing. Even Marie dared to ask him frequently for music, and he never refused her request. Three times he had taken Billy to some play that she wanted to see, and he had invited Marie, too, besides Aunt Hannah, which had pleased Billy very much. He had been at the same time so genial and so gallant that Billy had declared to Marie afterward that he did not seem like himself at all, but like some one else.

Marie had disagreed with her, it is true, and had said stiffly:

"I'm sure I thought he seemed very much like himself." But that had not changed Billy's opinion at all.

To Billy's mind, nothing but love could so have softened the stern Cyril she had known. She was, therefore, all the more careful these days to avoid a tete-a-tete with him, though she was not always successful, particularly owing to Marie's unaccountable perverseness in so often having letters to write or work to do, just when Billy most wanted her to make a safe third with herself and Cyril. It was upon such an occasion, after Marie had abruptly left them alone together, that Cyril had observed, a little sharply:

"Billy, I wish you wouldn't say again what you said ten minutes ago when Miss Marie was here."

"What was that?"

"A very silly reference to that old notion that you and every one else seem to have that I am a 'woman-hater.'"

Billy's heart skipped a beat. One thought, pounded through her brain and dinned itself into her ears—at all costs Cyril must not be allowed to say that which she so feared; he must be saved from himself.

"Woman-hater? Why, of course you're a woman-hater," she cried merrily. "I'm sure, I—I think it's lovely to be a woman-hater."

The man opened wide his eyes; then he frowned angrily.

"Nonsense, Billy, I know better. Besides, I'm in earnest, and I'm not a woman-hater."

"Oh, but every one says you are," chattered Billy. "And, after all, you know it IS distinguishing!"

With a disdainful exclamation the man sprang to his feet. For a time he paced the room in silence, watched by Billy's fearful eyes; then he came back and dropped into the low chair at Billy's side. His whole manner had undergone a complete change. He was almost shamefaced as he said:

"Billy, I suppose I might as well own up. I don't think I did think much of women until I saw—you."

Billy swallowed and wet her lips. She tried to speak; but before she could form the words the man went on with his remarks; and Billy did not know whether to be the more relieved or frightened thereat.

"But you see now it's different. That's why I don't like to sail any longer under false colors. There's been a change—a great and wonderful change that I hardly understand myself."

"That's it! You don't understand it, I'm sure," interposed Billy, feverishly. "It may not be such a change, after all. You may be deceiving yourself," she finished hopefully.

The man sighed.

"I can't wonder you think so, of course," he almost groaned. "I was afraid it would be like that. When one's been painted black all one's life, it's not easy to change one's color, of course."

"Oh, but I didn't say that black wasn't a very nice color," stammered Billy, a little wildly.

"Thank you." Cyril's heavy brows rose and fell the fraction of an inch. "Still, I must confess that just now I should prefer another shade."

He paused, and Billy cast distractedly about in her mind for a simple, natural change of subject. She had just decided to ask him what he thought of the condition of the Brittany peasants, when he questioned abruptly, and in a voice that was not quite steady:

"Billy, what should you say if I should tell you that the avowed woman-hater had strayed so far from the prescribed path as to—to like one woman well enough as to want to—marry her?"

The word was like a match to the gunpowder of Billy's fears. Her self-control was shattered instantly into bits.

"Marry? No, no, you wouldn't—you couldn't really be thinking of that," she babbled, growing red and white by turns. "Only think how a wife would—would b-bother you!"

"Bother me? When I loved her?"

"But just think—remember! She'd want cushions and rugs and curtains, and you don't like them; and she'd always be talking and laughing when you wanted quiet; and she—she'd want to drag you out to plays and parties and—and everywhere. Indeed, Cyril, I'm sure you'd never like a wife—long!" Billy stopped only because she had no breath with which to continue.

Cyril laughed a little grimly.

"You don't draw a very attractive picture, Billy. Still, I'm not afraid. I don't think this particular—wife would do any of those things—to trouble me."

"Oh, but you don't know, you can't tell," argued the girl. "Besides, you have had so little experience with women that you'd just be sure to make a mistake at first. You want to look around very carefully—very carefully, before you decide."

Eleanor H. Porter

"I have looked around, and very carefully, Billy. I know that in all the world there is just one woman for me."

Billy struggled to her feet. Mingled pain and terror looked from her eyes. She began to speak wildly, incoherently. She wondered afterward just what she would have said if Aunt Hannah had not come into the room at that moment and announced that Bertram was at the door to take her for a sleigh-ride if she cared to go.

"Of course she'll go," declared Cyril, promptly, answering for her. "It is time I was off anyhow." To Billy, he said in a low voice: "You haven't been very encouraging, little girl—in fact, you've been mighty discouraging. But some day—some other day, I'll try to make clear to you—many things."

Billy greeted Bertram very cordially. It was such a relief—his cheery, genial companionship! The air, too, was bracing, and all the world lay under a snow-white blanket of sparkling purity. Everything was so beautiful, so restful!

It was not surprising, perhaps, that the very frankness of Billy's joy misled Bertram a little. His blood tingled at her nearness, and his eyes grew deep and tender as he looked down at her happy face. But of all the eager words that were so near his lips, not one reached the girl's ears until the good-byes were said; then wistfully Bertram hazarded:

"Billy, don't you think, sometimes, that I'm gaining—just a little on that rival of mine—that music?"

Billy's face clouded. She shook her head gently.

"Bertram, please don't—when we've had such a beautiful hour together," she begged. "It troubles me. If you do, I can't go—again."

"But you shall go again," cried Bertram, bravely smiling straight into her eyes. "And there sha'n't ever anything in the world trouble you, either—that I can help!"

CHAPTER XXXIII

WILLIAM IS WORRIED

Billy's sleigh-ride had been due to the kindness of a belated winter storm that had surprised every one the last of March. After that, March, as if ashamed of her untoward behavior, donned her sweetest smiles and "went out" like the proverbial lamb. With the coming of April, and the stirring of life in the trees, Billy, too, began to be restless; and at the earliest possible moment she made her plans for her long anticipated "digging in the dirt."

Just here, much to her surprise, she met with wonderful assistance from Bertram. He seemed to know just when and where and how to dig, and he displayed suddenly a remarkable knowledge of landscape gardening. (That this knowledge was as recent in its acquirement as it was sudden in its display, Billy did not know.) Very learnedly he talked of perennials and annuals; and without hesitation he made out a list of flowering shrubs and plants that would give her a "succession of bloom throughout the season." His words and phrases smacked loudly of the very newest florists' catalogues, but Billy did not notice that. She only wondered at the seemingly exhaustless source of his wisdom.

"I suspect 'twould have been better if we'd begun things last fall," he told her frowningly one day. "But there's plenty we can do now anyway; and we'll put in some quick-growing things, just for this season, until we can get the more permanent things established."

And so they worked together, studying, scheming, ordering plants and seeds, their two heads close together above the gaily colored catalogues. Later there was the work itself to be done, and though strong men did the heavier part, there was yet plenty left for Billy's eager fingers—and for Bertram's. And if sometimes in the intimacy of seed-sowing and plant-setting, the touch of the slenderer fingers sent a thrill through the browner ones, Bertram made no sign. He was careful always to be the cheerful, helpful assistant—and that was all.

Billy, it is true, was a little disturbed at being quite so much with Bertram. She dreaded a repetition of some such words as had been uttered at the end of the sleigh-ride. She told herself that she had no right to grieve Bertram, to make it hard for him by being with him; but at the very next breath, she could but question; did she grieve him? Was it hard for him to have her with him? Then she would glance at his eager face and meet his buoyant smile—and answer "no." After that, for a time, at least, her fears would be less.

Systematically Billy avoided Cyril these days. She could not forget his promise to make many things clear to her some day. She thought she knew what he meant—that he would try to convince her (as she had tried to convince herself) that she would make a good wife for him.

Billy was very sure that if Cyril could be prevented from speaking his mind just now, his mind would change in time; hence her determination to give his mind that opportunity.

Billy's avoidance of Cyril was the more easily accomplished because she was for a time taking a complete rest from her music. The new songs had been finished and sent to the publishers. There was no excuse, therefore, for Cyril's coming to the house on that score; and, indeed, he seemed of his own accord to be making only infrequent visits now. Billy was pleased, particularly as Marie was not there to play third party. Marie had taken up her teaching again, much to Billy's distress.

"But I can't stay here always, like this," Marie had protested.

"But I should like to keep you!" Billy had responded, with no less decision.

Marie had been firm, however, and had gone, leaving the little house lonely without her.

Aside from her work in the garden Billy as resolutely avoided Bertram as she did Cyril. It was natural, therefore, that at this crisis she should turn to William with a peculiar feeling of restfulness. He, at least, would be safe, she told herself. So she frankly welcomed his every appearance, sung to him, played to him, and took long walks with him to see some wonderful bracelet or necklace that he had discovered in a dingy little curio-shop.

William was delighted. He was very fond of his namesake, and he had secretly chafed a little at the way his younger brothers had monopolized her attention. He was rejoiced now that she seemed to be turning to him for companionship; and very eagerly he accepted all the time she could give him.

William had, in truth, been growing more and more lonely ever since Billy's brief stay beneath his roof years before. Those few short weeks of her merry presence had shown him how very forlorn the house was without it. More and more sorrowfully during past years, his thoughts had gone back to the little white flannel bundle and to the dear hopes it had carried so long ago. If the boy had only lived, thought William, mournfully, there would not now have been that dreary silence in his home, and that sore ache in his heart.

Very soon after William had first seen Billy, he began to lay wonderful plans, and in every plan was Billy. She was not his child by flesh and blood, he acknowledged, but she was his by right of love and needed care. In fancy he looked straight down the years ahead, and everywhere he saw Billy, a loving, much-loved daughter, the joy of his life, the solace of his declining years.

To no one had William talked of this—and to no one did he show the bitterness of his grief when he saw his vision fade into nothingness through Billy's unchanging refusal to live in his home. Only he himself knew the heartache, the lonely-ness, the almost unbearable longing of the past winter months while Billy had lived at Hillside; and only he himself knew now the almost overwhelming joy that was his because of what he thought he saw in Billy's changed attitude toward himself.

Great as was William's joy, however, his caution was greater. He said nothing to Billy of his new hopes, though he did try to pave the way by dropping an occasional word about the loneliness of the Beacon Street house since she went away. There was something else, too, that caused William to be silent—what he thought he saw between Billy and Bertram. That Bertram was in love with Billy, he guessed; but that Billy was not in love with Bertram he very much feared. He hesitated almost to speak or move lest something he should say or do should, just at the critical moment, turn matters the wrong way. To William this

Eleanor H. Porter

marriage of Bertram and Billy was an ideal method of solving the problem, as of course Billy would come there to the house to live, and he would have his "daughter" after all. But as the days passed, and he could see no progress on Bertram's part, no change in Billy, he began to be seriously worried—and to show it.

CHAPTER XXXIV

CLASS DAY

Early in June Billy announced her intention of not going away at all that summer.

"I don't need it," she declared. "I have this cool, beautiful house, this air, this sunshine, this adorable view. Besides, I've got a scheme I mean to carry out."

There was some consternation among Billy's friends when they found out what this "scheme" was: sundry of Billy's humbler acquaintances were to share the house, the air, the sunshine, and the adorable view with her.

"But, my dear Billy," Bertram cried, aghast, "you don't mean to say that you are going to turn your beautiful little house into a fresh-air place for Boston's slum children!"

"Not a bit of it," smiled the girl, "though I'd like to, really, if I could," she added, perversely. "But this is quite another thing. It's no slum work, no charity. In the first place my guests aren't quite so poor as that, and they're much too proud to be reached by the avowed charity worker. But they need it just the same."

　　　　　Eleanor H. Porter

"But you haven't much spare room; have you?" questioned Bertram.

"No, unfortunately; so I shall have to take only two or three at a time, and keep them maybe a week or ten days. It's just a sugar plum, Bertram. Truly it is," she added whimsically, but with a tender light in her eyes.

"But who are these people?" Bertram's face had lost its look of shocked surprise, and his voice expressed genuine interest.

"Well, to begin with, there's Marie. She'll stay all summer and help me entertain my guests; at the same time her duties won't be arduous, and she'll get a little playtime herself. One week I'm going to have a little old maid who keeps a lodging house in the West End. For uncounted years she's been practically tied to a doorbell, with never a whole day to breathe free. I've made arrangements there for a sister to keep house a whole week, and I'm going to show this little old maid things she hasn't seen for years: the ocean, the green fields, and a summer play or two, perhaps.

"Then there's a little couple that live in a third-story flat in South Boston. They're young and like good times; but the man is on a small salary, and they have had lots of sickness. He's been out so much he can't take any vacation, and they wouldn't have any money to go anywhere if he could. Well, I'm going to have them a week. She'll be here all the time, and he'll come out at night, of course.

"Another one is a widow with six children. The children are already provided for by a fresh-air society, but the woman I'm going to take, and—and give her a whole week of food that she didn't have to cook herself. Another one is a woman who is not so very poor, but who has lost her baby, and is blue and discouraged. There are some children, too, one crippled, and a boy who says he's 'just lonesome.' And there are—really, Bertram, there is no end to them."

"I can well believe that," declared Bertram, with emphasis, "so far as your generous heart is concerned."

Billy colored and looked distressed.

"But it isn't generosity or charity at all, Bertram," she protested. "You are mistaken when you think it is—really! Why, I shall enjoy every bit of it just as well as they do—and better, perhaps."

"But you stay here—in the city—all summer for their sakes."

"What if I do? Besides, this isn't the real city," argued Billy, "with all these trees and lawns about one. And another thing," she added, leaning forward confidentially, "I might as well confess, Bertram, you couldn't hire me to leave the place this summer—not while all these things I planted are coming up!"

Bertram laughed; but for some reason he looked wonderfully happy as he turned away.

On the fifteenth of June Kate and her husband arrived from the West. A young brother of Mr. Hartwell's was to be graduated from Harvard, and Kate said they had come on to represent the family, as the elder Mr. and Mrs. Hartwell were not strong enough to undertake the journey. Kate was looking well and happy. She greeted Billy with effusive cordiality, and openly expressed her admiration of Hillside. She looked very keenly into her brothers' face, and seemed well pleased with the appearance of Cyril and Bertram, but not so much so with William's countenance.

"William does NOT look well," she declared one day when she and Billy were alone together.

"Sick? Uncle William sick? Oh, I hope not!" cried the girl.

"I don't know whether it's 'sick' or not," returned Mrs. Hartwell. "But it's something. He's troubled. I'm going to speak to him. He's worried over something; and he's grown terribly thin."

"But he's always thin," reasoned Billy.

"I know, but not like this—ever. You don't notice it, perhaps, or realize it, seeing him every day as you do. But I know something troubles him."

"Oh, I hope not," murmured Billy, with anxious eyes. "We don't want Uncle William troubled: we all love him too well."

Mrs. Hartwell did not at once reply; but for a long minute she thoughtfully studied Billy's face as it was bent above the sewing in Billy's hand. When she did speak she had changed the subject.

Young Hartwell was to deliver the Ivy Oration in the Stadium on Class Day, and all the Henshaws were looking eagerly forward to the occasion.

"You have seen the Stadium, of course," said Bertram to Billy, a few days before the anticipated Friday.

"Only from across the river."

"Is that so? And you've never been here Class Day, either. Good! Then you've got a treat in store. Just wait and see!"

And Billy waited—and she saw. Billy began to see, in fact, before Class Day. Young Hartwell was a popular fellow, and he was eager to have his friends meet Billy and the Henshaws. He was a member of the Institute of 1770, D. K. E., Stylus, Signet, Round Table, and Hasty Pudding Clubs, and nearly every one of these had some sort of function planned for Class-Day week. By the time the day itself arrived Billy was almost as excited as was young Hartwell himself.

It rained Class-Day morning, but at nine o'clock the sun came out and drove the clouds away, much to every one's delight. Billy's day began at noon with the spread given by the Hasty Pudding Club. Billy wondered afterward how many times that day remarks like these were made to her:

"You've been here Class Day before, of course. You've seen the confetti-throwing!... No? Well, you just wait!"

At ten minutes of four Billy and Mrs. Hartwell, with Mr. Hartwell and Bertram as escorts, entered the cool, echoing shadows under the Stadium, and then out in the sunlight they began to climb the broad steps to their seats.

"I wanted them high up, you see," explained Bertram, "because you can get the effect so much better. There, here we are!"

For the first time Billy turned and looked about her. She gave a low cry of delight.

"Oh, oh, how beautiful—how wonderfully beautiful!"

"You just wait!" crowed Bertram. "If you think this is beautiful, you just wait!"

Billy did not seem to hear him. Her eyes were sweeping the wonderful scene before her, and her face was aglow with delight.

First there was the great amphitheater itself. Only the wide curve of the horseshoe was roped off for to-day's audience. Beyond lay the two sides with their tier above tier of empty seats, almost dazzling in the sunshine. Within the roped-off curve the scene was of kaleidoscopic beauty. Charmingly gowned young women and carefully groomed young men were everywhere, stirring, chatting, laughing. Gay-colored parasols and flower-garden hats made here and there brilliant splashes of rainbow tints. Above was an almost cloudless canopy of blue, and at the far horizon, earth and sky met and made a picture that was like a wondrous painted curtain hung from heaven itself.

At the first sound of the distant band that told of the graduates' coming, Bertram said almost wistfully:

"Class Day is the only time when I feel 'out of it.' You see I'm the first male Henshaw for ages that hasn't been through Harvard; and to-day, you know, is the time when the old grads come back and do stunts like the kids—if they can (and some of them can all right!). They march in by classes ahead of the seniors, and vie with each other in giving their yells. You'll see Cyril and William, if your eyes are sharp enough—and you'll see them as you never saw them before."

Far down the green field Billy spied now the long black line of moving figures with a band in the lead. Nearer and nearer it came until, greeted by a mighty roar from thousands of throats, the leaders swept into the great bowl of the horseshoe curve.

And how they yelled and cheered—those men whose first

Class Day lay five, ten, fifteen, even twenty or more years behind them, as told by the banners which they so proudly carried. How they got their heads together and gave the "Rah! Rah! Rah!" with unswerving eyes on their leader! How they beat the air with their hats in time to their lusty shouts! And how the throngs above cheered and clapped in answer, until they almost split their throats—and did split their gloves—especially when the black-gowned seniors swept into view.

And when the curving line of black had become one solid mass of humanity that filled the bowl from side to side, the vast throng seated themselves, and a great hush fell while the Glee Club sang.

Young Hartwell proved to be a good speaker, and his ringing voice reached even the topmost tier of seats. Billy was charmed and interested. Everything she saw and heard was but a new source of enjoyment, and she had quite forgotten the thing for which she was to "wait," when she saw the ushers passing through the aisles with their baskets of many-hued packages of confetti and countless rolls of paper ribbon.

It began then, the merry war between the students below and the throng above. In a trice the air was filled with shimmering bits of red, blue, white, green, purple, pink, and yellow. From all directions fluttering streamers that showed every color of the rainbow, were flung to the breeze until, upheld by the supporting wires, they made a fairy lace work of marvelous beauty.

"Oh, oh, oh!" cried Billy, her eyes misty with emotion. "I think I never saw anything in my life so lovely!

"I thought you'd like it," gloried Bertram. "You know I said to wait!"

But even with this, Class Day for Billy was not finished. There was still Hartwell's own spread from six to eight, and after that there were the President's reception, and dancing in the Memorial Hall and in the Gymnasium. There was the Fairyland of the yard, too, softly aglow with moving throngs of beautiful women and gallant men. But what Billy remembered best of all was the exquisite harmony that came to her through the hushed night air when the Glee Club sang Fair Harvard on the steps of Holworthy Hall.

CHAPTER XXXV

SISTER KATE AGAIN

It was on the Sunday following Class Day that Mrs. Hartwell carried out her determination to "speak to William." The West had not taken from Kate her love of managing, and she thought she saw now a matter that sorely needed her guiding hand.

William's thin face, anxious looks, and nervous manner had troubled her ever since she came. Then one day, very suddenly, had come enlightenment: William was in love— and with Billy.

Mrs. Hartwell watched William very closely after that. She saw his eyes follow Billy fondly, yet anxiously. She saw his open joy at being with her, and at any little attention, word, or look that the girl gave him. She remembered, too, something that Bertram had said about William's grief because Billy would not live at the Strata. She thought she saw something else, also: that Billy was fond of William, but that William did not know it; hence his frequent troubled scrutiny of her face. Why these two should play at cross purposes Sister Kate could not understand. She smiled, however, confidently: they should not play at cross purposes much longer, she declared.

Eleanor H. Porter

On Sunday afternoon Kate asked her eldest brother to take her driving.

"Not a motor car; I want a horse—that will let me talk," she said.

"Certainly," agreed William, with a smile; but Bertram, who chanced to hear her, put in the sly comment: "As if ANY horse could prevent—that!"

On the drive Kate began to talk at once, but she did not plunge into the subject nearest her heart until she had adroitly led William into a glowing enumeration of Billy's many charming characteristics; then she said:

"William, why don't you take Billy home with you?"

William stirred uneasily as he always did when anything annoyed him.

"My dear Kate, there is nothing I should like better to do," he replied.

"Then why don't you do it?"

"I—hope to, sometime."

"But why not now?"

"I'm afraid Billy is not quite—ready."

"Nonsense! A young girl like that does not know her own mind lots of times. Just press the matter a little. Love will work wonders sometimes."

William blushed like a girl. To him her words had but one

meaning—Bertram's love for Billy. William had never spoken of this suspected love affair to any one. He had even thought that he was the only one that had discovered it. To hear his sister refer thus lightly to it came therefore in the nature of a shock to him.

"Then you have—seen it—too?" he stammered

"'Seen it, too,'" laughed Kate, with her confident eyes on William's flushed face, "I should say I had seen it! Any one could see it."

William blushed again. Love to him had always been something sacred; something that called for hushed voices and twilight. This merry discussion in the sunlight of even another's love was disconcerting.

"Now come, William," resumed Kate, after a moment; "speak to Billy, and have the matter settled once for all. It's worrying you. I can see it is."

Again William stirred uneasily.

"But, Kate, I can't do anything. I told you before; I don't believe Billy is—ready."

"Nonsense! Ask her."

"But Kate, a girl won't marry against her will!"

"I don't believe it is against her will."

"Kate! Honestly?"

"Honestly! I've watched her."

"Then I WILL speak," cried the man, his face alight, "if—if you think anything I can say would—help. There is nothing —nothing in all this world that I so desire, Kate, as to have that little girl back home. And of course that would do it. She'd live there, you know."

"Why, of—course," murmured Kate, with a puzzled frown. There was something in this last remark of William's that she did not quite understand. Surely he could not suppose that she had any idea that after he had married Billy they would go to live anywhere else;—she thought. For a moment she considered the matter vaguely; then she turned her attention to something else. She was the more ready to do this because she believed that she had said enough for the present: it was well to sow seeds, but it was also well to let them have a chance to grow, she told herself.

Mrs. Hartwell's next move was to speak to Billy, and she was careful to do this at once, so that she might pave the way for William.

She began her conversation with an ingratiating smile and the words:

"Well, Billy, I've been doing a little detective work on my own account."

"Detective work?"

"Yes; about William. You know I told you the other day how troubled and anxious he looked to me. Well, I've found out what's the matter."

"What is it?"

"Yourself."

"Myself! Why, Mrs. Hartwell, what can you mean?"

The elder lady smiled significantly.

"Oh, it's merely another case, my dear, of 'faint heart never won fair lady.' I've been helping on the faint heart; that's all."

"But I don't understand."

"No? I can't believe you quite mean that, my dear. Surely you must know how earnestly my brother William is longing for you to go back and live with him."

Like William, Billy flushed scarlet.

"Mrs. Hartwell, certainly no one could know better than YOURSELF why that is quite impossible," she frowned.

The other colored confusedly.

"I understand, of course, what you mean. And, Billy, I'll confess that I've been sorry lots of times, since, that I spoke as I did to you, particularly when I saw how it grieved my brother William to have you go away. If I blundered then, I'm sorry; and perhaps I did blunder. At all events, that is only the more reason now why I am so anxious to do what I can to rectify that old mistake, and plead William's suit."

To Mrs. Hartwell's blank amazement, Billy laughed outright.

"'William's suit'!" she quoted merrily. "Why, Mrs. Hartwell, there isn't any 'suit' to it. Uncle William doesn't want me to marry him!"

"Indeed he does."

Billy stopped laughing, and sat suddenly erect.

"MRS. HARTWELL!"

"Billy, is it possible that you did not know this?"

"Indeed I don't know it, and—excuse me, but I don't think you do, either."

"But I do. I've talked with him, and he's very much in earnest," urged Mrs. Hartwell, speaking very rapidly. "He says there's nothing in all the world that he so desires. And, Billy, you do care for him—I know you do!"

"Why, of course I care for him—but not—that way."

"But, Billy, think!" Mrs. Hartwell was very earnest now, and a little frightened. She felt that she must bring Billy to terms in some way now that William had been encouraged to put his fate to the test. "Just remember how good William has always been to you, and think what you have been, and may BE—if you only will—in his lonely life. Think of his great sorrow years ago. Think of this dreary waste of years between. Think how now his heart has turned to you for love and comfort and rest. Billy, you can't turn away!—you can't find it in your heart to turn away from that dear, good man who loves you so!" Mrs. Hartwell's voice shook effectively, and even her eyes looked through tears. Mentally she was congratulating herself: she had not supposed she could make so touching an appeal.

In the chair opposite the girl sat very still. She was pale, and her eyes showed a frightened questioning in their depths. For a long minute she said nothing, then she rose dazedly to her feet.

"Mrs. Hartwell, please do not speak of this to any one," she begged in a low voice. "I—I am taken quite by surprise. I shall have to think it out—alone."

Billy did not sleep well that night. Always before her eyes was the vision of William's face; and always in her ears was the echo of Mrs. Hartwell's words: "Remember how good William has always been to you. Think of his great sorrow years ago. Think of this dreary waste of years between. Think how now his heart has turned to you for love and comfort and rest."

For a time Billy tossed about on her bed trying to close her eyes to the vision and her ears to the echo. Then, finding that neither was possible, she set herself earnestly to thinking the matter out.

William loved her. Extraordinary as it seemed, such was the fact; Mrs. Hartwell said so. And now—what must she do; what could she do? She loved no one—of that she was very sure. She was even beginning to think that she would never love any one. There were Calderwell, Cyril, Bertram, to say nothing of sundry others, who had loved her, apparently, but whom she could not love. Such being the case, if she were, indeed, incapable of love herself, why should she not make the sacrifice of giving up her career, her independence, and in that way bring this great joy to Uncle William's heart?... Even as she said the "Uncle William" to herself, Billy bit her lip and realized that she must no longer say "Uncle" William—if she married him.

"If she married him." The words startled her. "If she married him."... Well, what of it? She would go to live at the Strata, of course; and there would be Cyril and Bertram. It might be awkward, and yet—she did not believe Cyril was in love with anything but his music; and as to Bertram—it was the same with Bertram and his painting, and he would soon forget that he had ever fancied he loved her. After that he would be simply a congenial friend and companion—a good comrade. As Billy thought of it, indeed, one of the pleasantest features of this marriage with William would be the delightful comradeship of her "brother," Bertram.

Billy dwelt then at some length on William's love for her, his longing for her presence, and his dreary years of loneliness .... And he was so good to her, she recollected; he had always been good to her. He was older, to be sure—much older than she; but, after all, it would not be so difficult, so very difficult, to learn to love him. At all events, whatever happened, she would have the supreme satisfaction of knowing that at least she had brought into dear Uncle—that is, into William's life the great peace and joy that only she could give.

It was almost dawn when Billy arrived at this not uncheerful state of prospective martyrdom. She turned over then with a sigh, and settled herself to sleep. She was relieved that she had decided the question. She was glad that she knew just what to say when William should speak. He was a dear, dear man, and she would not make it hard for him, she promised herself. She would be William's wife.

CHAPTER XXXVI

WILLIAM MEETS WITH A SURPRISE

In spite of his sister's confident assurance that the time was ripe for him to speak to Billy, William delayed some days before broaching the matter to her. His courage was not so good as it had been when he was talking with Kate. It seemed now, as it always had, a fearsome thing to try to hasten on this love affair between Billy and Bertram. He could not see, in spite of Kate's words, that Billy showed unmistakable evidence at all of being in love with his brother. The more he thought of it, in fact, the more he dreaded the carrying out of his promise to speak to his namesake.

What should he say, he asked himself. How could he word it? He could not very well accost her with: "Oh, Billy, I wish you'd please hurry up and marry Bertram, because then you'd come and live with me." Neither could he plead Bertram's cause directly. Quite probably Bertram would prefer to plead his own. Then, too, if Billy really was not in love with Bertram—what then? Might not his own untimely haste in the matter forever put an end to the chance of her caring for him?

It was, indeed, a delicate matter, and as William pondered it

Eleanor H. Porter

he wished himself well out of it, and that Kate had not spoken. But even as he formed the wish, William remembered with a thrill Kate's positive assertion that a word from him would do wonders, and that now was the time to utter it. He decided then that he would speak; that he must speak; but that at the same time he would proceed with a caution that would permit a hasty retreat if he saw that his words were not having the desired effect. He would begin with a frank confession of his grief at her leaving him, and of his longing for her return; then very gradually, if wisdom counseled it, he would go on to speak of Bertram's love for her, and of his own hope that she would make Bertram and all the Strata glad by loving him in return.

Mrs. Hartwell had returned to her Western home before William found just the opportunity for his talk with Billy. True to his belief that only hushed voices and twilight were fitting for such a subject, he waited until he found the girl early one evening alone on her vine-shaded veranda. He noticed that as he seated himself at her side she flushed a little and half started to rise, with a nervous fluttering of her hands, and a murmured "I'll call Aunt Hannah." It was then that with sudden courage, he resolved to speak.

"Billy, don't go," he said gently, with a touch of his hand on her arm. "There is something I want to say to you. I—I have wanted to say it for some time."

"Why, of—of course," stammered the girl, falling back in her seat. And again William noticed that odd fluttering of the slim little hands.

For a time no one spoke, then William began softly, his eyes on the distant sky-line still faintly aglow with the sunset's reflection.

"Billy, I want to tell you a story. Long years ago there was a man who had a happy home with a young wife and a tiny baby boy in it. I could not begin to tell you all the plans that man made for that baby boy. Such a great and good and wonderful being that tiny baby was one day to become. But the baby—went away, after a time, and carried with him all the plans—and he never came back. Behind him he left empty hearts that ached, and great bare rooms that seemed always to be echoing sighs and sobs. And then, one day, such a few years after, the young wife went to find her baby, and left the man all alone with the heart that ached and the great bare rooms that echoed sighs and sobs.

"Perhaps it was this—the bareness of the rooms—that made the man turn to his boyish passion for collecting things. He wanted to fill those rooms full, full!—so that the sighs and sobs could not be heard; and he wanted to fill his heart, too, with something that would still the ache. And he tried. Already he had his boyish treasures, and these he lined up in brave array, but his rooms still echoed, and his heart still ached; so he built more shelves and bought more cabinets, and set himself to filling them, hoping at the same time that he might fill all that dreary waste of hours outside of business—hours which once had been all too short to devote to the young wife and the baby boy.

"One by one the years passed, and one by one the shelves and the cabinets were filled. The man fancied, sometimes, that he had succeeded; but in his heart of hearts he knew that the ache was merely dulled, and that darkness had only to come to set the rooms once more to echoing the sighs and sobs. And then—but perhaps you are tired of the story, Billy." William turned with questioning eyes.

"No, oh, no," faltered Billy. "It is beautiful, but so—sad!"

"But the saddest part is done—I hope," said William, softly. "Let me tell you. A wonderful thing happened then. Suddenly, right out of a dull gray sky of hopelessness, dropped a little brown-eyed girl and a little gray cat. All over the house they frolicked, filling every nook and cranny with laughter and light and happiness. And then, like magic, the man lost the ache in his heart, and the rooms lost their echoing sighs and sobs. The man knew, then, that never again could he hope to fill his heart and life with senseless things of clay and metal. He knew that the one thing he wanted always near him was the little brown-eyed girl; and he hoped that he could keep her. But just as he was beginning to bask in this new light—it went out. As suddenly as they had come, the little brown-eyed girl and the gray cat went away. Why, the man did not know. He knew only that the ache had come back, doubly intense, and that the rooms were more gloomy than ever. And now, Billy,"—William's voice shook a little—"it is for you to finish the story. It is for you to say whether that man's heart shall ache on and on down to a lonely old age, and whether those rooms shall always echo the sighs and sobs of the past."

"And I will finish it," choked Billy, holding out both her hands. "It sha'n't ache—they sha'n't echo!"

The man leaned forward eagerly, unbelievingly, and caught the hands in his own.

"Billy, do you mean it? Then you will come?"

"Yes, yes! I didn't know—I didn't think. I never supposed it was like that! Of course I'll come!" And in a moment she was sobbing in his arms.

"Billy!" breathed William rapturously, as he touched his lips to her forehead. "My own little Billy!"

It was a few minutes later, when Billy was more calm, that William started to speak of Bertram. For a moment he had been tempted not to mention his brother, now that his own point had been won so surprisingly quick; but the new softness in Billy's face had encouraged him, and he did not like to let the occasion pass when a word from him might do so much for Bertram. His lips parted, but no words came— Billy herself had begun to speak.

"I'm sure I don't know why I'm crying," she stammered, dabbing her eyes with her round moist ball of a handerchief. "I hope when I'm your wife I'll learn to be more self-controlled. But you know I am young, and you'll have to be patient."

As once before at something Billy said, the world to William went suddenly mad. His head swam dizzily, and his throat tightened so that he could scarcely breathe. By sheer force of will he kept his arm about Billy's shoulder, and he prayed that she might not know how numb and cold it had grown. Even then he thought he could not have heard aright.

"Er—you said—" he questioned faintly.

"I say when I'm your wife I hope I'll learn to be more self-controlled," laughed Billy, nervously. "You see I just thought I ought to remind you that I am young, and that you'll have to be patient."

William stammered something—a hurried something; he wondered afterward what it was. That it must have been satisfactory to Billy was evident, for she began laughingly to talk again. What she said, William scarcely knew, though he was conscious of making an occasional vague reply. He was still floundering in a hopeless sea of confusion and dismay. His own desire was to get up and say good night at once. He

Eleanor H. Porter

wanted to be alone to think. He realized, however, with sickening force, that men do not propose and run away—if they are accepted. And he was accepted; he realized that, too, overwhelmingly. Then he tried to think how it had happened, what he had said; how she could so have misunderstood his meaning. This line of thought he abandoned quickly, however; it could do no good. But what could do good, he asked himself. What could he do?

With blinding force came the answer: he could do nothing. Billy cared for him. Billy had said "yes." Billy expected to be his wife. As if he could say to her now: "I beg your pardon, but 'twas all a mistake. *I* did not ask you to marry me."

Very valiantly then William summoned his wits and tried to act his part. He told himself, too, that it would not be a hard one; that he loved Billy dearly, and that he would try to make her happy. He winced a little at this thought, for he remembered suddenly how old he was—as if he, at his age, were a fit match for a girl of twenty-one!

And then he looked at Billy. The girl was plainly nervous. There was a deep flush on her cheeks and a brilliant sparkle in her eyes. She was talking rapidly—almost incoherently at times—and her voice was tremulous. Frequent little embarrassed laughs punctuated her sentences, and her fingers toyed with everything that came within reach. Some time before she had sprung to her feet and had turned on the electric lights; and when she came back she had not taken her old position at William's side, but had seated herself in a chair near by. All of which, according to William's eyes, meant the maidenly shyness of a girl who has just said "yes" to the man she loves.

William went home that night in a daze. To himself he said

that he had gone out in search of a daughter, and had come back with a wife.

CHAPTER XXXVII

"WILLIAM'S BROTHER"

It was decided that for the present, the engagement should not be known outside the family. The wedding would not take place immediately, William said, and it was just as well to keep the matter to themselves until plans were a little more definite.

The members of the family were told at once. Aunt Hannah said "Oh, my grief and conscience!" three times, and made matters scarcely better by adding apologetically: "Oh, of course it's all right, it's all right, only—" She did not finish her sentence, and William, who had told her the news, did not know whether he would have been more or less pleased if she had finished it.

Cyril received the information moodily, and lapsed at once into a fit of abstraction from which he roused himself hardly enough to offer perfunctory congratulations and best wishes.

Billy was a little puzzled at Cyril's behavior. She had been sure for some time that Cyril had ceased to care specially for her, even if he ever did fancy that he loved her. She had hoped to keep him for a friend, but of late she had been forced to question even his friendliness. He had, in fact, gone back almost to his old reserve and taciturn aloofness.

From the West, in response to William's news of the engagement, came a cordially pleased note in Kate's scrawling handwriting. Kate, indeed, seemed to be the only member of the family who was genuinely delighted with the coming marriage. As to Bertram—Bertram appeared to have aged years in a single night, so drawn and white was his face the morning after William had told him his plans.

William had dreaded most of all to tell Bertram. He was very sure that Bertram himself cared for Billy; and it was doubly hard because in William's own mind was a strong conviction that the younger man was decidedly the one for her. Realizing, however, that Bertram must be told, William chose a time for the telling when Bertram was smoking in his den in the twilight, with his face half hidden from sight.

Bertram said little—very little, that night; but in the morning he went straight to Billy.

Billy was shocked. She had never seen the smiling, self-reliant, debonair Bertram like this.

"Billy, is this true?" he demanded. The dull misery in his voice told Billy that he knew the answer before he asked the question.

"Yes, yes; but, Bertram, please—please don't take it like this!" she implored.

"How would you have me take it?"

"Why, just—just sensibly. You know I told you that—that the other never could be—never."

Eleanor H. Porter

"I know YOU said so; but I—believed otherwise."

"But I told you—I did not love you—that way."

Bertram winced. He rose to his feet abruptly.

"I know you did, Billy. I'm a fool, of course, to think that I could ever—change it. I shouldn't have come here, either, this morning. But I—had to. Good-by!" His face, as he held out his hand, was tragic with renunciation.

"Why, Bertram, you aren't going—now—like this!" cried the girl. "You've just come!"

The man turned almost impatiently.

"And do you think I can stay—like this? Billy, won't you say good-by?" he asked in a softer voice, again with outstretched hand.

Billy shook her head. She ignored the hand, and resolutely backed away.

"No, not like that. You are angry with me," she grieved. "Besides, you make it sound as if—if you were going away."

"I am going away."

"Bertram!" There was terror as well as dismay in Billy's voice.

Again the man turned sharply.

"Billy, why are you making this thing so hard for me?" he asked in despair. "Can't you see that I must go?"

"Indeed, I can't. And you mustn't go, either. There isn't any reason why you should," urged Billy, talking very fast, and working her fingers nervously. "Things are just the same as they were before—for you. I'm just going to marry William, but I wasn't ever going to marry you, so that doesn't change things any for you. Don't you see? Why, Bertram, you mustn't go away! There won't be anybody left. Cyril's going next week, you know; and if you go there won't be anybody left but William and me. Bertram, you mustn't go; don't you see? I should feel lost without—you!" Billy was almost crying now.

Bertram looked up quickly. An odd change had come to his face. For a moment he gazed silently into Billy's agitated countenance; then he asked in a low voice:

"Billy, did you think that after you and William were married I should still continue to live at—the Strata?"

"Why, of course you will!" cried the girl, indignantly. "Why, Bertram, you'll be my brother then—my real brother; and one of the very chiefest things I'm anticipating when I go there to live is the good times you and I will have together when I'm William's wife!"

Bertram drew in his breath audibly, and caught his lower lip between his teeth. With an abrupt movement he turned his back and walked to the window. For a full minute he stayed there, watched by the amazed, displeased eyes of the girl. When he came back he sat down quietly in the chair facing Billy. His countenance was grave and his eyes were a little troubled; but the haggard look of misery was quite gone.

"Billy," he began gently, "you must forgive my saying this, but—are you quite sure you—love William?"

Billy flushed with anger.

"You have no right to ask such a question. Of course I love William."

"Of course you do—we all love William. William is, in fact, a most lovable man. But William's wife should, perhaps, love him a little differently from—all of us."

"And she will, certainly," retorted the girl, with a quick lifting of her chin. "Bertram, I don't think you have any right to—to make such insinuations."

"And I won't make them any more," replied Bertram, gravely. "I just wanted you to make sure that you—knew."

"I shall make sure, and I shall know," said Billy, firmly—so firmly that it sounded almost as if she were trying to convince herself as well as others.

There was a long pause, then the man asked diffidently:

"And so you are very sure that—that you want me to—stay?"

"Indeed I do! Besides,—don't you remember?—there are all my people to be entertained. They must be taken to places, and given motor rides and picnics. You told me last week that you'd love to help me; but, of course, if you don't want to—"

"But I do want to," cried Bertram, heartily, a gleam of the old cheerfulness springing to his eyes. "I'm dying to!"

The girl looked up with quick distrust. For a moment she eyed him with bent brows. To her mind he had gone back to his old airy, hopeful light-heartedness. He was once more "only Bertram." She hesitated, then said with stern decision:

"Bertram, you know I want you, and you must know that I'm delighted to have you drop this silly notion of going away. But if this quick change means that you are staying with any idea that—that *I* shall change, then—then you must go. But if you will stay as WILLIAM'S BROTHER then—I'll be more than glad to have you."

"I'll stay—as William's brother," agreed Bertram; and Billy did not notice the quick indrawing of his breath nor the close shutting of his lips after the words were spoken.

Eleanor H. Porter

CHAPTER XXXVIII

THE ENGAGEMENT OF TWO

By the middle of July the routine of Billy's days was well established. Marie had been for a week a welcome addition to the family, and she was proving to be of invaluable aid in entertaining Billy's guests. The overworked widow and the little lodging-house keeper from the West End were enjoying Billy's hospitality now; and just to look at their beaming countenances was an inspiration, Billy said.

Cyril had gone abroad. Aunt Hannah was spending a week at the North Shore with friends. Bertram, true to his promise, was playing the gallant to Billy's guests; and so assiduous was he in his attentions that Billy at last remonstrated with him.

"But I didn't mean them to take ALL your time," she protested.

"Don't they like it? Do they see too much of me?" he demanded.

"No, no! They love it, of course. You must know that. Nobody else could give such beautiful times as you've given us. But it's yourself I'm thinking of. You're giving up all your time. Besides, I didn't mean to keep you here all summer, of course. You always go away some, you know, for a vacation."

"But I'm having a vacation here, doing this," laughed Bertram. "I'm sure I'm getting sea air down to the beaches and mountain air out to the Blue Hills. And as for excitement —if you can find anything more wildly exciting than it was yesterday when Miss Marie and I took the widow and the spinster lady on the Roller-coaster—just show it to me; that's all!"

Billy laughed.

"They told me about it—Marie in particular. She said you were lovely to them, and let them do every single thing they wanted to; and that half an hour after they got there they were like two children let out of school. Dear me, I wish I'd gone. I never stay at home that I don't miss something," she finished regretfully.

Bertram shrugged his shoulders.

"If it's Roller-coasters and Chute-the-chutes that you want, I fancy you'll get enough before the week is out," he sighed laughingly. "They said they'd like to go there to-morrow, please, when I asked them what we should do next. What surprises me is that they like such things—such hair-raising things. When I first saw them, black-gowned and stiff-backed, sitting in your little room here, I thought I should never dare offer them anything more wildly exciting than a church service or a lecture on psychology, with perhaps a band concert hinted at, provided the band could be properly instructed beforehand as to tempo and selections. But now— really, Billy, why do you suppose they have taken such a fancy to these kiddish stunts—those two staid women?"

Billy laughed, but her eyes softened.

"I don't know unless it's because all their lives they've been tied to such dead monotony that just the exhilaration of motion is bliss to them. But you won't always have to risk your neck and your temper in this fashion, Bertram. Next week my little couple from South Boston comes. She adores pictures and stuffed animals. You'll have to do the museums with her. Then there's little crippled Tommy—he'll be perfectly contented if you'll put him down where he can hear the band play. And all you'll have to do when that one stops is to pilot him to the next one. This IS good of you, Bertram, and I do thank you for it," finished Billy, fervently, just as Marie, the widow, and the "spinster lady" entered the room.

Billy told herself these days that she was very happy—very happy indeed. Was she not engaged to a good man, and did she not also have it in her power to make the long summer days a pleasure to many people? The fact that she had to tell herself that she was happy in order to convince herself that she was so, did not occur to Billy—yet.

Not long after Marie arrived, Billy told her of the engagement. William was at the house very frequently, and owing to the intimacy of Marie's relationship with the family Billy decided to tell her how matters stood. Marie's reception of the news was somewhat surprising. First she looked frightened.

"To William?—you are engaged to William?"

"Why—yes."

"But I thought—surely it was—don't you mean—Mr. Cyril?"

"No, I don't," laughed Billy. "And certainly I ought to know."

"And you don't—care for him?"

"I hope not—if I'm going to marry William."

So light was Billy's voice and manner that Marie dared one more question.

"And he—doesn't care—for you?"

"I hope not—if William is going to marry me," laughed Billy again.

"Oh-h!" breathed Marie, with an odd intonation of relief. "Then I'm glad—so glad! And I hope you'll be very, very happy, dear."

Billy looked into Marie's glowing face and was pleased: there seemed to be so few, so very few faces into which she had looked and found entire approbation of her engagement to William.

Billy saw a great deal of William now. He was always kind and considerate, and he tried to help her entertain her guests; but Billy, grateful as she was to him for his efforts, was relieved when he resigned his place to Bertram. Bertram did, indeed, know so much better how to do it. William tried to help her, too, about training her vines and rosebushes; but of course, even in this, he could not be expected to show quite the interest that Bertram manifested in every green shoot and opening bud, for he had not helped her plant them, as Bertram had.

Billy was a little troubled sometimes, that she did not feel more at ease with William. She thought it natural that she should feel a little diffident with him, in the face of his sudden change from an "uncle" to an accepted lover; but she did not see why she should be afraid of him—yet she was. She owned that to herself unhappily. And he was so good!—she owned that, too. He seemed not to have a thought in the world but for her comfort and happiness; and there was no end to the tactful little things he was always doing for her pleasure. He seemed, also, to have divined that she did not like to be kissed and caressed; and only occasionally did he kiss her, and then it was merely a sort of fatherly salute on her forehead—for which consideration Billy was grateful: Billy decided that she would not like to be kissed on the lips.

After some days of puzzling over the matter Billy concluded that it was self-consciousness that caused all the trouble. With William she was self-conscious. If she could only forget that she was some day to be William's wife, the old delightful comradeship would return, and she would be at ease again with him. In time, after she had become accustomed to the idea of marriage, it would not so confuse her, of course. She loved him dearly, and she wanted to make him happy; but for the present—just while she was "getting used to things"—she would try to forget, sometimes, that she was going to be William's wife.

Billy was happier now. She was always happier after she had thought things out to her own satisfaction. She turned with new zest to the entertainment of her guests; and with Bertram she planned many delightful trips for their pleasure. Bertram was a great comfort to her these days. Never, in word or look, could she see that he overstepped the role which he had promised to play—William's brother.

Billy went back to her music, too. A new melody was running through her head, and she longed to put it on paper. Already her first little "Group of Songs" had found friends, and Billy, to a very modest extent, was beginning to taste the sweets of fame.

Thus, by all these interests, did Billy try "to get used to things."

Eleanor H. Porter

CHAPTER XXXIX

A LITTLE PIECE OF PAPER

Of all Billy's guests, Marie was very plainly the happiest. She was a permanent guest, it is true, while the others came for only a week or two at a time; but it was not this, Billy decided, that had brought so brilliant a sparkle to Marie's eyes, so joyous a laugh to her lips. The joyousness was all the more noticeable, because heretofore Marie, while very sweet, had been also sad. Her big blue eyes had always carried a haunting shadow, and her step had lacked the spring belonging to youth and happiness. Certainly, Billy had never seen her like this before.

"Verily, Marie," she teased one day, "have you found an exhaustless supply of stockings to mend, or a never-done pudding to make—which?"

"Why? What do you mean?"

"Oh, nothing. I was only wondering just what had brought that new light to your eyes."

"Is there a new light?"

"There certainly is."

"It must be because I'm so happy, then," sighed Marie; "because you're so good to me."

"Is that all?"

"Isn't that enough?" Marie's tone was evasive.

"No." Billy shook her head mischievously. "Marie, what is it?"

"It's nothing—really, it's nothing," protested Marie, hurrying out of the room with a nervous laugh.

Billy frowned. She was suspicious before; she was sure now. In less than twelve hours' time came her opportunity. She was alone again with Marie.

"Marie, who is he?" she asked abruptly.

"He? Who?"

"The man who is to wear the stockings and eat the pudding."

The little music teacher flushed very red, but she managed to display something that might pass for surprise.

"BILLY!"

"Come, dear," coaxed Billy, winningly. "Tell me about it. I'm so interested!"

"But there isn't anything to tell—really there isn't."

"Who is he?"

"He isn't anybody—that is, he doesn't know he's anybody,"

amended Marie.

Billy laughed softly.

"Oh, doesn't he! Hasn't he ever shown—that he cared?"

"No; that is—perhaps he has, only I thought then—that it was—another girl."

"Another girl! So there's another girl in the case?"

"Yes. I mean, no," corrected Marie, suddenly beginning to realize what she was saying. "Really, it wasn't anything—it isn't anything!" she protested.

"Hm-m," murmured Billy, archly. "Oh, I'm getting on some! He did show, once, that he cared; but you thought it was another girl, and you coldly looked the other way. Now, there ISN'T any other girl, you find, and—Marie, tell me the rest!"

Marie shook her head emphatically, and pulled herself gently away from Billy's grasp.

"No, no, please!" she begged. "It really isn't anything. I'm sure I'm imagining it all!" she cried, as she ran away.

During the days that followed, Billy speculated not a little on Marie's half-told story, and wondered interestedly who the man might be. She questioned Marie once again, but the girl would tell nothing more; and, indeed, Billy was so occupied with her own perplexities that she had little time for those of other people.

To herself Billy was forced to own that she was not "getting used to things." She was still self-conscious with William;

she could not forget that she was one day to be his wife. She could not bring back the dear old freedom of comradeship with him.

Billy was alarmed now. She had begun to ask herself searching questions. What should she do if never, never should she get used to the idea of marrying William? How could she marry him if he was still "Uncle William," and never her dear lover in her eyes? Why had she not been wise enough and brave enough to tell him in the first place that she was not at all sure that she loved him, but that she would try to do so? Then when she had tried—as she had now—and failed, she could have told him honestly the truth, and it would not have been so great a shock to him as it must be now, if she should tell him.

Billy had remorsefully come to the conclusion that she could never love any man well enough to marry him, when one day so small a thing as a piece of paper fluttered into her vision, and showed her the fallacy of that idea.

It was a half-sheet of note paper, and it blew from Marie's balcony to the lawn below. Billy found it there later, and as she picked it up her eyes fell on a single name in Marie's handwriting inscribed half a dozen times as if the writer had musingly accompanied her thoughts with her pen; and the name was, "Marie Henshaw."

For a moment Billy stared at the name perplexedly—then in a flash came the remembrance of Marie's words; and Billy breathed: "Henshaw!—the man—BERTRAM!"

Billy dropped the paper then and fled. In her own room, behind locked doors, she sat down to think.

Bertram! It was he for whom Marie cared—HER Bertram!

Eleanor H. Porter

And then it came to Billy with staggering force that he was not HER Bertram at all. He never could be her Bertram now. He was—Marie's.

Billy was frightened then, so fierce was this strange new something that rose within her—this overpowering something that seemed to blot out all the world, and leave only— Bertram. She knew then, that it had always been Bertram to whom she had turned, though she had been blind to the cause of that turning. Always her plans had included him. Always she had been the happiest in his presence; never had she pictured him anywhere else but at her side. Certainly never had she pictured him as the devoted lover of another woman!... And she had not known what it all meant—poor blind child that she was!

Very resolutely now Billy set herself to looking matters squarely in the face. She understood it quite well. All summer Marie and Bertram had been thrown together. No wonder Marie had fallen in love with Bertram, and that he— Billy thought she comprehended now why Bertram had found it so easy for the last few weeks to be William's brother. She, of course, had been the "other girl" whom Marie had once feared that the man loved. It was all so clear —so woefully clear!

With an aching heart Billy asked herself what now was to be done. For herself, turn whichever way she could, she could see nothing but unhappiness. She determined, therefore, with Spartan fortitude, that to no one else would she bring equal unhappiness. She would be silent. Bertram and Marie loved each other. That matter was settled. As to William—Billy thought of the story William had told her of his lonely life,— of the plea he had made to her; and her heart ached. Whatever happened, William must be made happy. William must not be told. Her promise to William must be kept.

CHAPTER XL

WILLIAM PAYS A VISIT

Before September passed all Billy's friends said that her summer's self-appointed task had been too hard for her. In no other way could they account for the sad change that had come to her.

Undeniably Billy looked really ill. Always slender, she was shadow-like now. Her eyes had found again the wistful appeal of her girlhood, only now they carried something that was almost fear, as well. The rose-flush had gone from her cheeks, and pathetic little hollows had appeared, making the round young chin below look almost pointed. Certainly Billy did seem to be ill.

Late in September William went West on business. Incidentally he called to see his sister, Kate.

"Well, and how is everybody?" asked Kate, cheerily, after the greetings were over.

William sighed.

"Well, 'everybody,' to me, Kate, is pretty badly off. We're worried about Billy."

"Billy! You don't mean she's sick? Why, she's always been the picture of health!"

"I know she has; but she isn't now."

"What's the trouble?"

"That's what we don't know."

"You've had the doctor?"

"Of course; two or three of them—though much against Billy's will. But—they didn't help us."

"What did they say?"

"They could find nothing except perhaps a little temporary stomach trouble, or something of that kind, which they all agreed was no just cause for her present condition."

"But what did they say it was?"

"Why, they said it seemed like nervousness, or as if something was troubling her. They asked if she weren't under some sort of strain."

"Well, is she? Does anything trouble her?"

"Not that I know of. Anyhow, if there is anything, none of us can find out what it is."

Kate frowned. She threw a quick look into her brother's face.

"William," she began hesitatingly, "forgive me, but Billy is quite happy in—her engagement, I suppose."

The man flushed painfully, and sighed.

"I've thought of that, of course. In fact, it was the first thing I did think of. I even began to watch her rather closely, and once I—questioned her a little."

"What did she say?"

"She seemed so frightened and distressed that I didn't say much myself. I couldn't. I had but just begun when her eyes filled with tears, and she asked me in a frightened little voice if she had done anything to displease me, anything to make me unhappy; and she seemed so anxious and grieved and dismayed that I should even question her, that I had to stop."

"What has she done this summer? Where has she been?"

"She hasn't been anywhere. Didn't I write you? She's kept open house for a lot of her less fortunate friends—a sort of vacation home, you know; and—and I must say she's given them a world of happiness, too."

"But wasn't that hard for her?"

"It didn't seem to be. She appeared to enjoy it immensely, particularly at first. Of course she had plenty of help, and that wonderful little Miss Hawthorn has been a host in herself. They're all gone now, anyway, except Miss Hawthorn."

"But Billy must have had the care and the excitement."

"Perhaps—to a certain extent. Though not much, after all. You see Bertram, too, has given up his summer to them, and has been playing the devoted escort to the whole bunch. Indeed, for the last few weeks of it, since Billy began to seem so ill, he and Miss Hawthorn have schemed to take all the care from Billy, and they have done the whole thing together."

"But what HAS Billy done to make her like this?"

"I don't know. She's done lots for me, in all sorts of ways—cataloguing my curios, you know, and going with me to hunt up things. In fact, she seems the happiest when she IS doing something for me. It's come to be a sort of mania with her, I'm afraid—to do something for me. Kate, I'm really worried. What do you suppose is the matter?"

Kate shook her head. The puzzled frown had come back to her face.

"I can't imagine," she began slowly. "Of course, when I told her you loved her and—"

"When you told her wha-at?" exploded the usually low-voiced William, with sudden sharpness.

"When I told her that you loved her, William. You see, I—"

William sprang to his feet.

"Told her that I loved her!" he cried, aghast. "Good heavens, Kate, do you mean to say that YOU told her THAT."

"Why, y-yes."

"And may I ask where you got your information?"

"Why, William Henshaw, what a question! I got it from yourself, of course," defended Kate.

"From ME!" William's face expressed sheer amazement.

"Certainly; on that drive when I was East in June," returned Kate, with dignity. "YOU evidently have forgotten it, but I have not. You told me very frankly how much you thought of her, and how you longed to have her back there with you, but that she didn't seem to be ready to come. I was sorry for you, and I wanted to do something to help, particularly as it might have been my fault, partly, that she went away, in the first place."

William lifted his head.

"What do you mean?"

"Why, nothing, only that I—I told her a little of how—how upsetting her arrival had been to everything, and of how much you had done for her, and put yourself out. I said it so she'd appreciate things, of course, but she took it quite differently from what I had intended she should take it, and seemed quite cut up about it. Then she went away in that wily, impulsive fashion."

William bit his lip, but he did not speak. Kate was plunging on feverishly, and in the face of the greater revelation he let the lesser one drop.

"And so that's why I was particularly anxious to bring things around right again," continued Kate. "And that's why I spoke. I thought I'd seen how things were, and on the drive I said so. Then is when I advised you to speak to Billy; but you declared that Billy wasn't ready, and that you couldn't make a girl marry against her will. NOW don't you recollect it?"

A great light of understanding broke over William's face. He started to speak, but something evidently stayed the words on his lips. With controlled deliberation he turned and sat

Eleanor H. Porter

down. Then he said:

"Kate, will you kindly tell me just what you DID do?"

"Why, I didn't do so very much. I just tried to help, that's all. After I talked with you, and advised you to ask Billy right away to marry you, I went to her. I thought she cared for you already, anyway; but I just wanted to tell her how very much it was to you, and so sort of pave the way. And now comes the part that I started to tell you a little while ago when you caught me up so sharply. I was going to say that when I told Billy this, she appeared to be surprised, and almost frightened. You see, she hadn't known you cared for her, after all, and so I had a chance to help and make it plain to her how you did love her, so that when you spoke everything would be all right. There, that's all. You see I didn't do so very much."

"'So very much'!" groaned William, starting to his feet. "Great Scott!"

"Why, William, what do you mean? Where are you going?"

"I'm going—to—Billy," retorted William with slow distinctness. "And I'm going to try to get there—before—you—CAN!" And with this extraordinary shot—for William—he left the house.

William went to Billy as fast as steam could carry him. He found her in her little drawing-room listlessly watching with Aunt Hannah the game of chess that Bertram and Marie were playing.

"Billy, you poor, dear child, come here," he said abruptly, as soon as the excitement of his unexpected arrival had passed. "I want to talk to you." And he led the way to the veranda which he knew would be silent and deserted.

"To talk to—me?" murmured Billy, as she wonderingly came to his side, a startled questioning in her wide dark eyes.

Eleanor H. Porter

CHAPTER XLI

THE CROOKED MADE STRAIGHT

William did not re-enter the house after his talk with Billy on the veranda.

"I will go down the steps and around by the rose garden to the street, dear," he said. "I'd rather not go in now. Just make my adieus, please, and say that I couldn't stay any longer. And now—good-by." His eyes as they looked down at her, were moist and very tender. His lips trembled a little, but they smiled, and there was a look of new-born peace and joy on his face.

Billy, too, was smiling, though wistfully. The frightened questioning had gone from her eyes, leaving only infinite tenderness.

"You are sure it—it is all right—now?" she stammered.

"Very sure, little girl; and it's the first time it has been right for weeks. Billy, that was very dear of you, and I love you for it; but think how near—how perilously near you came to lifelong misery!"

"But I thought—you wanted me—so much," she smiled shyly.

"And I did, and I do—for a daughter. You don't doubt that NOW?"

"No, oh, no," laughed Billy, softly; and to her face came a happy look of relief as she finished: "And I'll be so glad to be—the daughter!"

For some minutes after the man had gone, Billy stood by the steps where he had left her. She was still there when Bertram came to the veranda door and spoke to her.

"Billy, I saw William go by the window, so I knew you were alone. May I speak to you?"

The girl turned with a start.

"Why, of course! What is it?—but I thought you were playing. Where is Marie?"

"The game is finished; besides—Billy, why are you always asking me lately where Marie is, as if I were her keeper, or she mine?" he demanded, with a touch of nervous irritation.

"Why, nothing, Bertram," smiled Billy, a little wearily; "only that you were playing together a few minutes ago, and I wondered where she had gone."

"'A few minutes ago'!" echoed Bertram with sudden bitterness. "Evidently the time passed swiftly with you, Billy. William was out here MORE than an hour."

"Why—Bertram!"

"Yes, I know. I've no business to say that, of course," sighed the man; "but, Billy, that's why I came out—because I must speak to you this once. Won't you come and sit down, please?" he implored despairingly.

"Why, Bertram," murmured Billy again, faintly, as she turned toward the vine-shaded corner and sat down. Her eyes were startled. A swift color had come to her cheeks.

"Billy," began the man, in a sternly controlled voice, "please let me speak this once, and don't try to stop me. You may think, for a moment, that it's disloyal to William if you listen; but it isn't. There's this much due to me—that you let me speak now. Billy, I can't stand it. I've tried, but it's no use. I've got to go away, and it's right that I should. I'm not the only one that thinks so, either. Marie does, too."

"MARIE!"

"Yes. I talked it all over with her. She's known for a long time how it's been with me; how I cared—for you."

"Marie! You've told Marie that?" gasped Billy.

"Yes. Surely you don't mind Marie's knowing," went on Bertram, dejectedly. "And she's been so good to me, and tried to—help me."

Bertram was not looking at Billy now. If he had been he would have seen the incredulous joy come into her face. His eyes were moodily fixed on the floor.

"And so, Billy, I've come to tell you. I'm going away," he continued, after a moment. "I've got to go. I thought once, when I first talked with you of William, that you didn't know your own heart; that you didn't really care for him. I was even fool enough to think that—that it would be I to whom you'd turn—some day. And so I stayed. But I stayed honorably, Billy! YOU know that! You know that I haven't once forgotten—not once, that I was only William's brother. I promised you I'd be that—and I have been; haven't I?"

Billy nodded silently. Her face was turned away.

"But, Billy, I can't do it any longer. I've got to ask for my promise back, and then, of course, I can't stay."

"But you—you don't have to go—away," murmured the girl, faintly.

Bertram sprang to his feet. His face was white.

"Billy," he cried, standing tall and straight before her, "Billy, I love every touch of your hand, every glance of your eye, every word that falls from your lips. Do you think I can stay —now? I want my promise back! When I'm no longer William's brother—then I'll go!"

"But you don't have to have it back—that is, you don't have to have it at all," stammered Billy, flushing adorably. She, too, was on her feet now.

"Billy, what do you mean?"

"Don't you see? I—I HAVE turned," she faltered breathlessly, holding out both her hands.

Even then, in spite of the great light that leaped to his eyes, Bertram advanced only a single step.

"But—William?" he questioned, unbelievingly.

"It WAS a mistake, just as you thought. We know now— both of us. We don't either of us care for the other—that way. And—Bertram, I think it HAS been you—all the time, only I didn't know!"

"Billy, Billy!" choked Bertram in a voice shaken with emotion. He opened his arms then, wide—and Billy walked straight into them.

CHAPTER XLII

THE "END OF THE STORY"

It was two days after Billy's new happiness had come to her that Cyril came home. He went very soon to see Billy.

The girl was surprised at the change in his appearance. He had grown thin and haggard looking, and his eyes were somber. He moved restlessly about the room for a time, finally seating himself at the piano and letting his fingers slip from one mournful little melody to another. Then, with a discordant crash, he turned.

"Billy, do you think any girl would marry—me?" he demanded.

"Why, Cyril!"

"There, now, please don't begin that," he begged fretfully. "I realize, of course, that I'm a very unlikely subject for matrimony. You made me understand that clearly enough last winter!"

"Last—winter?"

Cyril raised his eyebrows.

Eleanor H. Porter

"Oh, I came to you for a little encouragement, and to make a confession," he said. "I made the confession—but I didn't get the encouragement."

Billy changed color. She thought she knew what he meant, but at the same time she couldn't understand why he should wish to refer to that conversation now.

"A—confession?" she repeated, hesitatingly.

"Yes. I told you that I'd begun to doubt my being such a woman-hater, after all. I intimated that YOU'D begun the softening process, and that then I'd found a certain other young woman who had—well, who had kept up the good work."

"Oh!" cried Billy suddenly, with a peculiar intonation. "Oh-h!" Then she laughed softly.

"Well, that was the confession," resumed Cyril. "Then I came out flat-footed and said that I wanted to marry her—but there is where I didn't get the encouragement!"

"Indeed! I'm afraid I wasn't very considerate," stammered Billy.

"No, you weren't," agreed Cyril, moodily. "I didn't know but now—" his voice softened a little—"with this new happiness of yours and Bertram's that—you might find a little encouragement for me."

"And I will," cried Billy, promptly. "Tell me about her."

"I did—last winter," reproached the man, "and you were sure I was deceiving myself. You drew the gloomiest sort of picture of the misery I would take with a wife."

"I did?" Billy was laughing very merrily now.

"Yes. You said she'd always be talking and laughing when I wanted to be quiet, and that she'd want to drag me out to parties and plays when I wanted to stay at home; and—oh, lots of things. I tried to make it clear to you that—that this little woman wasn't that sort. But I couldn't," finished Cyril, gloomily.

"But of course she isn't," declared Billy, with quick sympathy. "I—I didn't know—WHAT—I was—talking about," she added with emphatic distinctness. Then she smiled to think how little Cyril knew how very true those words were. "Tell me about her," she begged again. "I know she must be very lovely and brilliant, and of course a wonderful musician. YOU couldn't choose any one else!"

To her surprise Cyril turned abruptly and began to play again. A nervous little staccato scherzo fell from his fingers, but it dropped almost at once into a quieter melody, and ended with something that sounded very much like the last strain of "Home, Sweet Home." Then he wheeled about on the piano stool.

"Billy, that's exactly where you're wrong—I DON'T want that kind of wife. I don't want a brilliant one, and—now, Billy, this sounds like horrible heresy, I know, but it's true—I don't care whether she can play, or not; but I should prefer that she shouldn't play—much!"

"Why, Cyril Henshaw!—and you, with your music! As if you could be contented with a woman like that!"

"Oh, I want her to like music, of course," modified Cyril; "but I don't care to have her MAKE it. Billy, do you know? You'll laugh, of course, but my picture of a wife is always one thing: a room with a table and a shaded lamp, and a little woman beside it with the light on her hair, and a great, basket of sewing beside her. You see I AM domestic!" he finished a little defiantly.

"I should say you were," laughed Billy. "And have you found her?—this little woman who is to do nothing but sit and sew in the circle of the shaded lamp?"

"Yes, I've found her, but I'm not at all sure she's found me. That's where I want your help. Oh, I don't mean, of course," he added, "that she's got to sit under that lamp all the time. It's only that—that I hope she likes that sort of thing."

"And—does she?"

"Yes; that is, I think she does," smiled Cyril. "Anyhow, she told me once that—that the things she liked best to do in all the world were to mend stockings and to make puddings."

Billy sprang to her feet with a little cry. Now, indeed, had Cyril kept his promise and made "many things clear" to her.

"Cyril, come here," she cried tremulously, leading the way to the open veranda door. The next moment Cyril was looking across the lawn to the little summerhouse in the midst of Billy's rose garden. In full view within the summerhouse sat Marie—sewing.

"Go, Cyril; she's waiting for you," smiled Billy, mistily. "The light's only the sun, to be sure, and maybe there isn't a whole basket of sewing there. But—SHE'S there!"

"You've—guessed, then!" breathed Cyril.

"I've not guessed—I know. And—it's all right."

"You mean—?" Only Cyril's pleading eyes finished the question.

"Yes, I'm sure she does," nodded Billy. And then she added under her breath as the man passed swiftly down the steps: "'Marie Henshaw' indeed! So 'twas Cyril all the time—and never Bertram—who was the inspiration of that bit of paper give-away!"

When she turned back into the room she came face to face with Bertram.

"I spoke, dear, but you didn't hear," he said, as he hurried forward with outstretched hands.

"Bertram," greeted Billy, with surprising irrelevance, "'and they all lived happily ever after'—they DID! Isn't that always the ending to the story—a love story?"

"Of course," said Bertram with emphasis;—"OUR love story!"

"And theirs," supplemented Billy, softly; but Bertram did not hear that.

ABOUT THE AUTHOR

Eleanor Hodgman Porter (December 19, 1868 – May 21, 1920) was an American novelist.

Born in Littleton, New Hampshire, Eleanor Hodgman trained as a singer but later turned to writing. In 1892 she married John Lyman Porter and moved to Massachusetts. Porter mainly wrote children's literature, for example three Miss Billy books, Cross currents [1928], The turn of the tide [1928] and Six Star Ranch [1916].

Her most famous novel is Pollyanna (1913), later followed by a sequel, Pollyanna Grows Up (1915). Her adult novels include The Story of Marco (1920), Just David (1915), The Road to Understanding (1916), Oh Money Money (1917), Dawn (1918), Keith's Dark Tower (1919), Mary Marie (1920), Sister Sue (1921), short stories include Money, Love and Kate (1924) and Little Pardner (1927).

She died in Cambridge, Massachusetts in 1920.

Other books by this author

Just David

Mary Marie

Miss Billy Married

Miss Billy's Decision

Oh, Money! Money!

Dawn

Pollyanna

Pollyanna Grows Up

Eleanor H. Porter

Choose from Thousands of 1stWorldLibrary Classics By

A. M. Barnard
Ada Leverson
Adolphus William Ward
Aesop
Agatha Christie
Alexander Aaronsohn
Alexander Kielland
Alexandre Dumas
Alfred Gatty
Alfred Ollivant
Alice Duer Miller
Alice Turner Curtis
Alice Dunbar
Allen Chapman
Alleyne Ireland
Ambrose Bierce
Amelia E. Barr
Amory H. Bradford
Andrew Lang
Andrew McFarland Davis
Andy Adams
Angela Brazil
Anna Alice Chapin
Anna Sewell
Annie Besant
Annie Hamilton Donnell
Annie Payson Call
Annie Roe Carr
Annonaymous
Anton Chekhov
Archibald Lee Fletcher
Arnold Bennett
Arthur C. Benson
Arthur Conan Doyle
Arthur M. Winfield
Arthur Ransome
Arthur Schnitzler
Arthur Train
Atticus
B.H. Baden-Powell
B. M. Bower
B. C. Chatterjee
Baroness Emmuska Orczy
Baroness Orczy
Basil King
Bayard Taylor
Ben Macomber
Bertha Muzzy Bower
Bjornstjerne Bjornson

Booth Tarkington
Boyd Cable
Bram Stoker
C. Collodi
C. E. Orr
C. M. Ingleby
Carolyn Wells
Catherine Parr Traill
Charles A. Eastman
Charles Amory Beach
Charles Dickens
Charles Dudley Warner
Charles Farrar Browne
Charles Ives
Charles Kingsley
Charles Klein
Charles Hanson Towne
Charles Lathrop Pack
Charles Romyn Dake
Charles Whibley
Charles Willing Beale
Charlotte M. Braeme
Charlotte M. Yonge
Charlotte Perkins Stetson
Clair W. Hayes
Clarence Day Jr.
Clarence E. Mulford
Clemence Housman
Confucius
Coningsby Dawson
Cornelis DeWitt Wilcox
Cyril Burleigh
D. H. Lawrence
Daniel Defoe
David Garnett
Dinah Craik
Don Carlos Janes
Donald Keyhoe
Dorothy Kilner
Dougan Clark
Douglas Fairbanks
E. Nesbit
E. P. Roe
E. Phillips Oppenheim
E. S. Brooks
Earl Barnes
Edgar Rice Burroughs
Edith Van Dyne
Edith Wharton

Edward Everett Hale
Edward J. O'Biren
Edward S. Ellis
Edwin L. Arnold
Eleanor Atkins
Eleanor Hallowell Abbott
Eliot Gregory
Elizabeth Gaskell
Elizabeth McCracken
Elizabeth Von Arnim
Ellem Key
Emerson Hough
Emilie F. Carlen
Emily Bronte
Emily Dickinson
Enid Bagnold
Enilor Macartney Lane
Erasmus W. Jones
Ernie Howard Pie
Ethel May Dell
Ethel Turner
Ethel Watts Mumford
Eugene Sue
Eugenie Foa
Eugene Wood
Eustace Hale Ball
Evelyn Everett-green
Everard Cotes
F. H. Cheley
F. J. Cross
F. Marion Crawford
Fannie E. Newberry
Federick Austin Ogg
Ferdinand Ossendowski
Fergus Hume
Florence A. Kilpatrick
Fremont B. Deering
Francis Bacon
Francis Darwin
Frances Hodgson Burnett
Frances Parkinson Keyes
Frank Gee Patchin
Frank Harris
Frank Jewett Mather
Frank L. Packard
Frank V. Webster
Frederic Stewart Isham
Frederick Trevor Hill
Frederick Winslow Taylor

Friedrich Kerst
Friedrich Nietzsche
Fyodor Dostoyevsky
G.A. Henty
G.K. Chesterton
Gabrielle E. Jackson
Garrett P. Serviss
Gaston Leroux
George A. Warren
George Ade
Geroge Bernard Shaw
George Cary Eggleston
George Durston
George Ebers
George Eliot
George Gissing
George MacDonald
George Meredith
George Orwell
George Sylvester Viereck
George Tucker
George W. Cable
George Wharton James
Gertrude Atherton
Gordon Casserly
Grace E. King
Grace Gallatin
Grace Greenwood
Grant Allen
Guillermo A. Sherwell
Gulielma Zollinger
Gustav Flaubert
H. A. Cody
H. B. Irving
H. C. Bailey
H. G. Wells
H. H. Munro
H. Irving Hancock
H. R. Naylor
H. Rider Haggard
H. W. C. Davis
Haldeman Julius
Hall Caine
Hamilton Wright Mabie
Hans Christian Andersen
Harold Avery
Harold McGrath
Harriet Beecher Stowe
Harry Castlemon
Harry Coghill
Harry Houidini

Hayden Carruth
Helent Hunt Jackson
Helen Nicolay
Hendrik Conscience
Hendy David Thoreau
Henri Barbusse
Henrik Ibsen
Henry Adams
Henry Ford
Henry Frost
Henry James
Henry Jones Ford
Henry Seton Merriman
Henry W Longfellow
Herbert A. Giles
Herbert Carter
Herbert N. Casson
Herman Hesse
Hildegard G. Frey
Homer
Honore De Balzac
Horace B. Day
Horace Walpole
Horatio Alger Jr.
Howard Pyle
Howard R. Garis
Hugh Lofting
Hugh Walpole
Humphry Ward
Ian Maclaren
Inez Haynes Gillmore
Irving Bacheller
Isabel Cecilia Williams
Isabel Hornibrook
Israel Abrahams
Ivan Turgenev
J. G.Austin
J. Henri Fabre
J. M. Barrie
J. M. Walsh
J. Macdonald Oxley
J. R. Miller
J. S. Fletcher
J. S. Knowles
J. Storer Clouston
J. W. Duffield
Jack London
Jacob Abbott
James Allen
James Andrews
James Baldwin

James Branch Cabell
James DeMille
James Joyce
James Lane Allen
James Lane Allen
James Oliver Curwood
James Oppenheim
James Otis
James R. Driscoll
Jane Abbott
Jane Austen
Jane L. Stewart
Janet Aldridge
Jens Peter Jacobsen
Jerome K. Jerome
Jessie Graham Flower
John Buchan
John Burroughs
John Cournos
John F. Kennedy
John Gay
John Glasworthy
John Habberton
John Joy Bell
John Kendrick Bangs
John Milton
John Philip Sousa
John Taintor Foote
Jonas Lauritz Idemil Lie
Jonathan Swift
Joseph A. Altsheler
Joseph Carey
Joseph Conrad
Joseph E. Badger Jr
Joseph Hergesheimer
Joseph Jacobs
Jules Vernes
Julian Hawthrone
Julie A Lippmann
Justin Huntly McCarthy
Kakuzo Okakura
Karle Wilson Baker
Kate Chopin
Kenneth Grahame
Kenneth McGaffey
Kate Langley Bosher
Kate Langley Bosher
Katherine Cecil Thurston
Katherine Stokes
L. A. Abbot
L. T. Meade

L. Frank Baum
Latta Griswold
Laura Dent Crane
Laura Lee Hope
Laurence Housman
Lawrence Beasley
Leo Tolstoy
Leonid Andreyev
Lewis Carroll
Lewis Sperry Chafer
Lilian Bell
Lloyd Osbourne
Louis Hughes
Louis Joseph Vance
Louis Tracy
Louisa May Alcott
Lucy Fitch Perkins
Lucy Maud Montgomery
Luther Benson
Lydia Miller Middleton
Lyndon Orr
M. Corvus
M. H. Adams
Margaret E. Sangster
Margret Howth
Margaret Vandercook
Margaret W. Hungerford
Margret Penrose
Maria Edgeworth
Maria Thompson Daviess
Mariano Azuela
Marion Polk Angellotti
Mark Overton
Mark Twain
Mary Austin
Mary Catherine Crowley
Mary Cole
Mary Hastings Bradley
Mary Roberts Rinehart
Mary Rowlandson
M. Wollstonecraft Shelley
Maud Lindsay
Max Beerbohm
Myra Kelly
Nathaniel Hawthrone
Nicolo Machiavelli
O. F. Walton
Oscar Wilde
Owen Johnson
P.G. Wodehouse
Paul and Mabel Thorne

Paul G. Tomlinson
Paul Severing
Percy Brebner
Percy Keese Fitzhugh
Peter B. Kyne
Plato
Quincy Allen
R. Derby Holmes
R. L. Stevenson
R. S. Ball
Rabindranath Tagore
Rahul Alvares
Ralph Bonehill
Ralph Henry Barbour
Ralph Victor
Ralph Waldo Emmerson
Rene Descartes
Ray Cummings
Rex Beach
Rex E. Beach
Richard Harding Davis
Richard Jefferies
Richard Le Gallienne
Robert Barr
Robert Frost
Robert Gordon Anderson
Robert L. Drake
Robert Lansing
Robert Lynd
Robert Michael Ballantyne
Robert W. Chambers
Rosa Nouchette Carey
Rudyard Kipling
Saint Augustine
Samuel B. Allison
Samuel Hopkins Adams
Sarah Bernhardt
Sarah C. Hallowell
Selma Lagerlof
Sherwood Anderson
Sigmund Freud
Standish O'Grady
Stanley Weyman
Stella Benson
Stella M. Francis
Stephen Crane
Stewart Edward White
Stijn Streuvels
Swami Abhedananda
Swami Parmananda
T. S. Ackland

T. S. Arthur
The Princess Der Ling
Thomas A. Janvier
Thomas A Kempis
Thomas Anderton
Thomas Bailey Aldrich
Thomas Bulfinch
Thomas De Quincey
Thomas Dixon
Thomas H. Huxley
Thomas Hardy
Thomas More
Thornton W. Burgess
U. S. Grant
Upton Sinclair
Valentine Williams
Various Authors
Vaughan Kester
Victor Appleton
Victor G. Durham
Victoria Cross
Virginia Woolf
Wadsworth Camp
Walter Camp
Walter Scott
Washington Irving
Wilbur Lawton
Wilkie Collins
Willa Cather
Willard F. Baker
William Dean Howells
William le Queux
W. Makepeace Thackeray
William W. Walter
William Shakespeare
Winston Churchill
Yei Theodora Ozaki
Yogi Ramacharaka
Young E. Allison
Zane Grey